Almost forgotten stories

HERMAN CHARLES BOSMAN

Almost forgotten stories

HOWARD TIMMINS PUBLISHERS

United Kingdom · Southern & East Africa
North America · Australia · New Zealand

HOWARD TIMMINS PUBLISHERS

Box 66, Aylesbury, HP21 7QA, Bucks. U.K.
Box 94, Cape Town 8000, S.A.
Box 880, Salisbury, Zimbabwe/Rhodesia.
Box 20051, Nairobi, Kenya.
Box 337, Sparta, New Jersey, 07871, U.S.A.
Box 876, Oakville, Ontario, L6J 5CS, Canada.
Box U1902, Perth, 6001, Western Australia.
Box 3457, Wellington, New Zealand.

ISBN 0 86978 167 7

Published by Howard Timmins (Pty) Ltd. S.A. 1979.
Designed & Printed by Cape & Transvaal Printers (Pty) Ltd. Cape Town.

Acknowledgements

The advent of *Almost Forgotten Stories* has been a somewhat unusual team event in that without the rallying force of its captain, the late Herman Charles Bosman, there could have been neither an event nor a team. But he was a fine thing to happen to South African letters; and in the process, he left this strangely varied collection of stories throwing into perspective some of the more bizarre aspects of his life.

After Bosman, my next appreciation goes to his widow and copyright-holder, Helena Lake, who warned me that she would remain strictly neutral throughout the experiment leading to this publication; but who—simply because she is Helena—could never be anything other than a source of energy and encouragement in ways she could not possibly be aware of.

I thank:

His friends Aegidius Jean Blignaut and the late Leon Feldberg—the two editors for whom Herman Bosman worked on a full-time basis who generously gave their approval to the *Sunday Express* experiment without raising a fee.

His pupil, disciple and unofficial literary executor, Lionel Abrahams, and Brian Lello and Robin Short—all editors of magazines who published the later stories and contributed fresh information about them.

Mr James S Winters and staff of the Johannesburg Reference Library.

The Humanities Research Center, Austin, Texas, from whose collection the story "The recognising blues" is drawn.

Paul Roos and the whole DALRO organization who xeroxed the original collection with their compliments—and smiled.

The media who gave this collection its initial public exposure.

The *Sunday Express* under the imaginative editorship of Rex Gibson and his team: Koos Viviers, Adrian Monteath, Ray Woodley, Richard Smith, Carol Lazar, Cathy Ruhmer and Paula Bradley. Their patience and enthusiasm made this endeavour not only worthwhile, but fun.

The English Service of the SABC under Ronnie Wilson, namely: Patricia Kerr, Marilyn Verster and Noreen Alexander of *Woman's World*, Will Bernard of *Radio Today* and Christopher Prior of *Audiomix*.

Springbok Radio: Timothy Bungey, Martin Woolf, Anne-Marie Muller and Michele Booyzen of *Women's Forum*.

The *External Service of the SABC*: Shirley Veal and Colin Houston.

Liliane Gigante-Paletta, freelance broadcaster for *Radio RSA* and *Springbok Radio*.

SATV: Graham Stuart, Athalie Brett and Nicki Hadfield of *Countrywide*.

The readers.

The serious ones who early in the experiment assessed the stories and gave me their comments: Professor Leon Hugo of UNISA, the Afrikaans poet Jeanne Goosen, journalist Doreen Levine, film-makers Ashley Lazarus, Jans Rautenbach and Gordon Vorster (also poet-painter, Bosman's disciple and drinking-mate), Colin Melville (book reviewer), Dr Carl Biccard Jeppe (naturalist, author and psychiatrist) and George Howard (Bosman's friend of twenty years) who took the stigma out of "barrel-scraping" for me.

Finally, the *un*serious readers: Bosman's "future ages".

When Herman Bosman said, "Leave it to the future ages to decide. They never go wrong," he spoke, I believe, in universalities. That they would one day lobby for the publication of some of his almost forgotten stories, never entered his head. But if in that place where all good writers go, he should receive the news as did the drum man in his story "The kafir-drum", then I believe he would say, "That sort of news is worth getting".

Compiler's Note

During the course of my research into the life of Herman Charles Bosman I had the fun of reading a number of short stories I had never seen before. Many of them had been languishing in the almost forgotten periodicals of the 1930s, while others from the forties and later had been excluded from permanent collections by eyes more critical than mine. (I make no apologies for being enormously prejudiced: I am a confirmed Bosmanophile.)

They span over twenty years of Bosman's adult writing career, include well over a dozen Schalk Lourens stories, some veld stories not related by Schalk Lourens, one Pretoria Central Prison story and a few Johannesburg ones—the latter of which may strike his readers as an alarming departure from his accustomed style.

These are not really new perspectives of one of South Africa's best loved writers, so much as almost forgotten ones of the man he was. Like the pupil of an eye constricting to accommodate light, they need time and exposure to fit the legend he became. And allowing that they might make Bosman more controversial, they cannot make him less universal.

Since the 1930s he has observed the socio-political scene, holding a mirror up to life in stories that relate not only to the microcosm under scrutiny, but to the human condition. Like radar, they have the property of scanning the humour threshold of his readers and zeroing in on the relevant level.

When I began to research his life I was asked by the Humanities Research Center at Austin, Texas (where the Bosman papers are lodged) whether I intended to do a data biography or an interpretative work. The short answer was "a bit of both". For early on I could see that Bosman drew no distinction between what an artist lived and what he created. So far as he was concerned the one was an extension of the other, and his advice on the matter was quite straightforward: "If you have any poetry inside you, go into the world and live it. The verses will write themselves."

Those pink and blue slips I had filled in for periodicals from the local reference library had yielded a double dividend: there were those encounters with "new" stories, and then there was the intriguing task of matching them to the events in Bosman's life.

For three years I had the adventure of trailing him around a paperchase of contradictory information through his own self-constructed smoke-screen. Actually, I should have considered myself warned.

In his story "The Kafir drum" (in *Unto Dust*) Bosman made a point of having his Black drum man suspect the efficacy of the new White telegraph operator because, not only is it important to have the right kind of person to send and receive news, but also the right person to tell news to.

This statement was more central to Bosman's thinking than most people realise, for I have known him to tell several different versions of the same story to different people, varying it according to the person concerned—or simply according to the way he felt.

So there are a number of misconceptions about Bosman's life—especially among people who knew him.

But then, as his pupil Lionel Abrahams put it: "Regarding history, Herman Charles Bosman put 'the poet's embroidered lie' above the carefully authenticated factual account. He was not only more willing to hear the first than the second, but readier to believe it too." I consider this to be one of the most telling statements about Bosman, and on it, I structured my biography of him *Sunflower to the Sun*.

In *Spotlight* magazine, along with the last Schalk Lourens story to appear in English during his lifetime, Bosman wrote a typically Bosmanesque autobiographical note:

"I was born in Kuils River about fifteen miles from

Cape Town, on February 3, 1905. A few years ago I revisited my birthplace. But there were no landmarks that I recognised. Nobody there had heard of me either.

"The most important educational influences in my life have been Jeppe High School, Witwatersrand University and unpropitious circumstances, the latter still acting as my mentor.

"After I had qualified as a school-teacher the Transvaal Education Department, apparently with the intention of doing me a disservice, appointed me to a Bushveld school in the Groot Marico. The disservice was to the Bushveld school. But while I was no good as a teacher I found in the Marico a pattern of life offering infinite riches in literary material.

"From school-teaching I turned to journalism. It took me ten years on Fleet Street to learn that I wasn't any good at that either. I should have learned quicker . . ."

Whilst I shall always regret my lack of direct exposure to Bosman's embroidered lie, it has given me the opportunity—I refuse to call it an *advantage*—of setting the record straight and filling in a few details. Like those about the "unpropitious circumstances" that acted as his mentor.

At the age of twenty Herman Bosman acquired a teaching diploma and a wife, in that order. On Friday, 21 February 1926 he borrowed £5 from Vera Sawyer, a young insurance clerk, gave his age as twenty-six, and married her under the name of Herbert Charles Boswell, leaving for his teaching post in the Marico the following Sunday without having consummated the marriage.

He returned for the July holidays with a hunting rifle, the weapon with which—in a moment of diminished responsibility—he mortally wounded his step-brother David Russell. He was given the death sentence, later commuted to eight years with hard labour, of which he eventually served three years and nine months at Pretoria Central Prison.

One difference between autobiography and biography is selectivity. If Bosman's version is based on an "embroidered lie" or two, mine is biased by this business of setting the record straight and filling in a couple of omissions.

In the light of hindsight, no responsible summary of the life of Herman Bosman, however lighthearted, would be complete without reference to Ellie Beemer, the young Jewess, incarnated in his slim volume of erotica *The Blue Princess*. Her rejection of him provoked its stinging dedication, and those vengeful gestures visited on her family in the shape of two stories in this volume, "Rita's marriage" and "Heloise's teeth". Similarly, no playful account—no matter how serious its aspirations—could overlook his second wife Ellaleen Manson, who began by inspiring the resoundingly beautiful lines:

"I sing of the morning I who have seen
Only the afternoons.
My westering heart is sunset stained
But white where the languorous lips have been
Of Ellaleen."

and thereafter launched them on a path of destruction which left him impotent (physically and spiritually) and exacted from her the ultimate price—her life.

Unless they were included in those "unpropitious circumstances still acting as his mentor", I can see that Bosman (quite correctly) just did not think his *Spotlight* autobiography the right place to make mention of any of the women in his life. Even those he might have considered propitious circumstances. Certainly not Helena who gave him back his words, and certainly not his "veld maiden"—that phantom love, whom, in one guise or another, he wooed in an ongoing love affair for all of his literary life.

Gerald Clarke says of writers: "Besides being given to wiping away their past, they are prone to fabrication. Mark Twain could never resist a good story about himself even if he had to make it up." Nor, may I add, could Bosman.

So you may not be surprised to hear that the ten years he claimed to have been a Fleet Street journalist were actually six. (He was in London from early 1934 to early 1940.) As to that successful publishing venture of which he often spoke, the Arden Godbold Press, nowhere in the annals of institutions documenting such statistics in the United Kingdom for this period can I find any trace of it. But I do know he resided at that address, vacating it abruptly after World War II without paying the rent and leaving his effects to be disposed of for £1 10s.

Much later, the gentle Helena, with whom he spent his last and most productive years, was his bewildered but uncomplaining accomplice in the elaborate lengths to which he went, straining an already ailing budget to the limit to convince the Receiver of Revenue that he was really a most successful author, who ought, therefore, to be assessed in a higher tax bracket

"The poet's embroidered lie," then, illumined Bosman's life with an essential truth far more potent than any apparent one. The apparent truth, after all, is relevant only as a frame of reference, which is our reason for relating these stories, wherever possible, to the chronological events in his life.

But facts are not to be worshipped. Just treated with respect. And not too much of that, either.

According to Bosman, unless an experience was illumined with trueness of vision, it could never be anything more than a fact recounted—no matter how authentic. But if it were truly *imagined*, then it could not fail to ring true—no matter how far-fetched.

If I were asked how much of Bosman's writing was true in the sense "how much was based on personal experience", I should be bound to reply, "A great deal." But if the same question were phrased in respect of the profundities of the word "truth", then my response could only be: "According to me—*all* of Bosman is true."

Valerie Rosenberg

Table of Contents

Publisher's Note

If the spelling of certain words in *Almost Forgotten Stories* differs erratically from story to story, it is because we set out to reproduce these individually as closely as possible to the original form in the magazines from which they were drawn. Bosman's earlier preferences were to spell the words "kaffir" with one "f" and "Afrikaner" with a "d", both of which he changed in later years. These differences might then be said to mirror the socio-political literary vogue of the times.

On to Freedom

The best way to present this collection of some of Herman Bosman's almost forgotten stories would be in chronological order related to his development. Those published for the first time posthumously, however, cannot without reference to the original manuscript, be dated with anything more than an educated guess. We are also deliberately deviating from the strict chronological order in two cases—the stories at the beginning and the end.

We start with On to freedom *for a reason I think Herman Bosman would have liked. Just for fun.*

It was first published on 24 July 1937 in the South African Opinion *under the editorship of Bernard Sachs. Bosman was then living in London with his second wife Ella Manson, and had reverted from his post-prison pen-name Herman Malan to H. C. Bosman.*

On to freedom *was written more than three years after he left South Africa. That makes this story about forty-odd years old. Or young.*

How we could tell that Gawie Prinsloo had been changed by his experiences on the diggings—Oom Schalk Lourens said—was when he came back from the diamond fields wearing a tie.

It was sad to see a young man altered so much by a few months of pick and shovel work on a claim. We came to the conclusion, however, that it wasn't the time he had spent on his claim with the pick and shovel that had changed Gawie Prinsloo: he must have got changed like that during those periods in which he didn't have a shovel in his hand, and the sweat wasn't dripping off him, and when he wasn't on his claim, even.

And judging by the way he had altered, it would seem that during much of Gawie Prinsloo's stay on the diggings he was not on the claim.

Of course, it was not a new thing in the Bushveld for a

young man to go to the diggings, fresh and unspoilt and God-fearing, and to come back different. Often at the Nagmaal the predikant would utter warnings about the dangers of the diamond fields; he would speak in solemn tones about what he called the false glitter of the alluvial diggings, and about the vanity of its carnal shows and sinful worldly riches. But it is just the unfortunate way of the world that many young men, who in the ordinary course would never have thought of leaving Marico, packed up and went to the diggings after they heard some of the things the predikant said: about the wild sort of life that was led there, and about the evils of suddenly-acquired wealth.

The predikant was on occasion very outspoken in dealing with the shameful things that took place on the diggings, and it was noticeable that at such times certain members of his congregation would shuffle their feet and get restless at his language. And only afterwards the predikant would discover that the reason they were restless was because they wanted to be off to the diggings.

I can still remember a remark that Wynand Oosthuizen once made in regard to this matter. It was when we were preparing to leave Zeerust after the Nagmaal.

"As you all know," Wynand Oosthuizen said, "My farm is situated right up against the Limpopo, and I live there alone. Consequently, I have much time in which to think. And I have thought about this question of the predikant and the young men and the diamond diggings. Yes, I have given it much thought. And I perceive that there is only one way in which the predikant will be able to get people to stay away from the diamond fields: he must say that the diamond fields are a lot like heaven."

We looked at Wynand Oosthuizen, wondering. It seemed to do queer things to a man, living alone like that beside the Limpopo.

Because we made no answer, Wynand Oosthuizen thought, apparently, that we hadn't understood what he was saying.

"You see," he went on, "After every Nagmaal I have observed that there is a big rush to the diamond diggings. That is because the predikant talks so much about the wickedness of life on the diggings; how the diamond fields are like Babylon, and how vice and evil flourish there, and how people make money there and then forget all about their duty to the church. Now, if the predikant were to say that the diggings are exactly like the Kingdom of heaven, nobody would want to go. No, nobody at all."

Wynand Oosthuizen winked, then, and set his hat at a slant and strode across to his ox-wagon. In silence, shaking our heads, we watched him getting ready to trek back to the Limpopo.

To do some more thinking, no doubt.

Then there was this matter of Gawie Prinsloo. As I have said, he was more changed than any other man that I had ever seen come back from the diggings. And I had seen many of them come back. Some came back with money that they didn't quite know what to do with: there seemed so much of it. Others came back penniless. One man whom I knew very well was reduced to selling his wagon and oxen on the diggings; and he returned to the Marico on foot, singing.

But Gawie Prinsloo was the only man who had ever come back from the diggings wearing a tie. What was more, it was a red tie; and Gawie Prinsloo said that he was wearing it for a political reason.

It was some time before I realised what Gawie Prinsloo meant by this. Then I proceeded to tell him about politics in the old days. Things were much better then, I said, and much simpler. Politics was concerned only with the question as to which man was going to be president.

"And if the wrong man got elected," I said to Gawie, very pointedly, "you merely inspanned and trekked out of the country. You didn't put on a red tie and walk about talking the sort of thing that you are talking now."

Gawie thought that over for a little while. Then he said

that it was cowardly to inspan and trek away from a difficulty. He explained that the right thing to do was to face a problem and to find a solution to it. It was easy to see, he said, how this spirit of trekking away had produced a race of men with weak characters and unenlightened minds.

Naturally, I asked him what he meant by a statement like that. I told him that in the past I had on several occasions trekked out of both the Transvaal and the Free State because I disapproved of the Presidents.

"Yes, Oom Schalk," Gawie said, "and look at you."

From that remark, thoughtlessly uttered on a summer afternoon, you can see how much the diggings had altered Gawie Prinsloo.

Afterwards we found out that there were other points about Gawie's new politics besides the wearing of a red tie. For instance, he held views about kafirs that nobody in the Bushveld had ever heard of before. He spoke a great deal about freedom, and in between mentioning what a good thing freedom was he would mumble something to the effect that in the Marico the kafirs weren't being treated right.

But, of course, it was quite a while before we discovered the extent to which Gawie Prinsloo's mind had been influenced by this kind of politics. He introduced us to it gradually, as though he was afraid of the shock it might give us if he acquainted us with all his opinions right away.

One day, however, in the home of Jasper Steyn, the ouderling, a number of farmers questioned Gawie Prinsloo closely on his beliefs, and you can imagine the sensation that was caused when he admitted that, in his view, a kafir was just as good as a white man.

"Do you really mean to say," Jasper Steyn, the ouderling, asked, choosing his words very carefully, "That you can't see any important difference between a kafir and a white man?"

"No," Gawie Prinsloo answered, "There is only a difference of colour, and that doesn't count."

Several of us burst out laughing at that; the ouderling rocked in his chair from side to side; you could hear him laughing right across in the next district, almost.

"Would you say," the ouderling went on, wiping the tears out of his eyes, "Would you say that there is no difference between me and a kafir? Would you say, for instance, that I am just a white kafir?"

"Yes," Gawie Prinsloo responded, promptly, "But that's what I thought about you even before I went to the diggings."

Subsequently, others took up the task of questioning Gawie Prinsloo. After he had got over his first sort of difference, however, there was no stopping him; he embarked on a long speech about justice and human rights and liberty; and what he kept on stressing all the time was what he called the wrongs of the kafirs.

It was easy to see that Gawie Prinsloo had been associating with a very questionable type of person on the diggings.

And because we knew that it was the diamond diggings that had led him astray we extended a great deal of tolerance towards his unusual utterances. We treated him as somebody who was not altogether responsible for what he said. In this way it became quite a fashionable pastime in the Marico for people to listen to Gawie Prinsloo talk. And he would talk by the hour about the way the kafirs were being oppressed.

"Look, Gawie," I said to him once. "Why do you tell only the white people about the injustice that is being inflicted on the kafirs? Why don't you go and tell the kafirs about what is being done to them?"

Gawie told me that he had already done so.

"I have gone among the kafirs" he said, "And I have told them about their wrongs."

But he admitted that his talks didn't seem to do much good, somehow; because the kafirs just went on smoking dagga—inhaling it through water, he said.

"And when I have told them about their wrongs and

about freedom they have laughed," Gawie explained, looking very puzzled. "Loudly."

So the months passed, and Gawie Prinsloo's red tie got
crinkled and faded-looking, and when Nagmaal came round
again he was still in exactly the same position in regard to
his politics; he still spoke fervently about justice for the
kafirs, and he had not yet brought anybody round to his
way of thinking. Moreover, he was no longer considered to
be amusing. People began to remark that it was annoying to
have to listen to his saying the same sort of thing over and
over again; they also hinted that it was about time he left the
Bushveld.

It was then that Wynand Oosthuizen, once more coming
to Zeerust for the Nagmaal, encountered Gawie Prinsloo
and his faded red tie and his politics. Several of us were
present at this meeting. By this time Gawie Prinsloo was
slightly desperate with his message. He had grown so used
to people not taking him seriously any more, that he had
given up reasoning with them in a calm way. So it was in a
markedly aggressive manner that he approached Wynand
Oosthuizen.

"The kafirs?" Gawie Prinsloo called out to Wynand.
"The kafirs aren't getting justice in the Marico. And a kafir
is just as good as you are."

Gawie Prinsloo started to walk away, then: but Wynand
Oosthuizen pulled him back—by his neck tie.

"Say that again," Wynand demanded.

Nothing if not fearless, Gawie repeated what he had said,
and a lot more besides.

Contrary to what we had expected, Wynand Oosthuizen
did not get annoyed. Nor did he laugh. Instead, he pushed
back his hat and looked intently at the young man with the
washed-out red tie.

"This is something new," he said slowly, "I haven't heard
that point of view before. And I can't tell whether you are
right or wrong. But I have got an idea. My farm is in the far
north, on the Limpopo, and I live there alone. I do a lot of

thinking there. You come and stay with me until the next Nagmaal, and we will think this question out together."

We were accustomed to Wynand Oosthuizen acting on occasion, in a singular fashion; it was well-known that the loneliness of his life by the Limpopo made his outlook different from that of most people. So we were not surprised at the nature of the invitation that he extended to Gawie Prinsloo. Nor were we surprised at Gawie Prinsloo's acceptance. For that matter, Gawie could not very well have done anything else: Wynand Oosthuizen was holding him so firmly by the tie.

"I will come with you," Gawie Prinsloo said, "But I know that I am right."

Thus, it was that they met in Zeerust and arranged to travel together to the Limpopo, to study the new politics about freedom and about equal rights for the kafirs— Wynand Oosthuizen, the lonely thinker, and Gawie Prinsloo, the young firebrand.

They agreed to meet again in church; at the Nagmaal, and to trek away as soon as possible after the service was over.

And I often wondered, subsequently, to what extent it was the predikant's sermon that had influenced two men who had planned to sojourn by the Limpopo and think of freedom. Because, in the morning, after the Nagmaal service, when Wynand Oosthuizen trekked away in his ox-wagon, Gawie Prinsloo was with him, and together they travelled the long and dusty road that led south, away from the thorn-trees of the Low Veld, to the diggings.

In Church

As a result of shooting his step-brother, Herman Bosman was detained in Pretoria Central Prison from November 1926 to August 1930. When he emerged he began to earn his living as a writer using his post-prison pen-name Herman Malan (derived from his mother's maiden name).

In church *is the first Bushveld story of this period—not related by Oom Schalk Lourens—that I have been able to trace. It was published on 2 January 1931 in the* Sjambok *(edited by Stephen Black) in the section* Life as revealed by fiction, *the same month as Bosman's first Schalk Lourens story* Makapan's caves *appeared in the Bosman-Blignaut literary monthly magazine the* Touleier.

Unlike Makapan's caves, *Bosman himself did not rate* In church *highly enough to include in his first collection of short stories* Mafeking Road. *In the interest of scholarship, however, it is the earliest indication in print of one of several veld themes he was to develop and polish over the years.*

Inside the school-room at Droogtebult there was the smell of cheap scent and stale powder mixed with sweat. The room was crowded on that Sunday morning, for a church service between the quarterly Nagmaals was an unusual event. There were present members of both Dutch churches, the Hervormde and the Gereformeerde, and the minister gave out only psalms, as he did not wish to antagonise the Doppers, who do not sing hymns.

Gerhardina Brink sat at the end of a row of school-benches. In that same row were her father and mother and her younger brothers and sisters. Gerhardina was the eldest of Thys Brink's children. She was sixteen. But already there was a fullness about her breasts and a maturity of development about her hips that elsewhere would be associated

with a woman much older than Gerhardina. The Bushveld
sun, ripening the kaffir-corn and the mealies, also ripened
the women very early, perhaps even before their time.
Already there had been young men who had courted Thys
Brink's daughter. There was the new school teacher, for
instance, who had come often to the farm and had sat up
with Gerhardina. But lately he had stayed away. It was
rumoured that he had applied to the Education Department
for a transfer to a school on the Highveld. They said that the
Bushveld climate did not agree with him.

While they were singing "Prys den Heer", Gerhardina
looked up from the book and encountered the gaze of the
school teacher. She had tried often during the service to
catch his eye, but always he had seemed to look past her.
But now there was no doubt about it. She had looked at
him at the same time that he had looked at her. Yes, he had
seen her, right enough . . . and all he did was to turn his
head away quickly and stare at something on the wall.
Suddenly Gerhardina felt a sickness within her. She heard
her father's voice droning the words of the psalm through
his beard. She saw Lena van Heerden glance at her strangely
and she blushed. She watched the minister putting slips of
paper in his Bible for place-marks. And all the time within
her was that terribly sick feeling.

She was relieved when the singing was over and she
could sit down again.

The minister was a young man who had only recently
qualified at the Potchefstroom Theological Seminary. He
was obviously nervous. He cleared his throat frequently and
stuttered even in reading the text. But the people to whom
he preached had a respect for all ministers. It was a reve-
rence that stretched back for many generations. It was older
than the Transvaal Republic. It was older than the Great
Trek. It was older than van Riebeeck. So now though the
minister stuttered and was nervous, the congregation did
not notice it.

"Sing, O barren, thou that didst not hear," he read.

"Break forth into singing and cry aloud, thou that didst not travail with child."

Gerhardina listened to these words. Somehow, she felt that she understood what those words meant, in a way that the minister could not understand them. She felt that it was just as though she had all at once become an old woman. The minister went on to talk about Isaiah, but she did not hear him. Again she glanced hurriedly at the school teacher, but he must have expected something like that, because his face was still turned away from her; and he was still studying that same part of the wall. The minister kept, talking, his nervousness beginning to wear off. Near the back a baby in arms started crying. It was a thin, pitiful sort of wail, and everybody turned round, as though they had never before heard a child cry. The mother rocked the baby to and fro in an effort to soothe it, but without success; she then walked out and stood in the sun in front of the door and nuzzled the child at her breast. A number of men near the door turned round and watched the operation idly.

"Thou that didst not travail with child," Gerhardina murmured to herself. She wondered if Lena van Heerden really had looked at her in a peculiar way, or if she had only imagined it. But there was no imagination about the way in which the teacher had purposely tried to avoid her.

Then she looked at her father and mother. She wondered how many times she had seen her father sit just that way in church, his shoulders hunched forward, his eyes half-closed, his black coat—which with age was becoming green in places—sprinkled at the collar with dandruff. Her mother had a handkerchief up to her eyes. There never yet had been a sermon preached that did not move her mother.

Gerhardina was pleased when the last psalm had been sung and the minister had pronounced the blessing. She walked on alone to the mule-cart which was standing under a thorn-tree. Her parents remained around the school building for a while, talking to different people. Also, her father was anxious to get in a word with the minister, because if people saw him conversing with the minister in an intimate kind of way it would help his chances of getting nominated as ouderling. Her brothers and sisters stayed with their parents, but Gerhardina wanted to be alone.

"I saw that school teacher," her father said when they get into the cart, "he was talking to Frikkie Haasbroek. When I came along he slunk away like a dog that steals fat. He doesn't come to see you any more, either. If he thinks we're not good enough for him, he can . . ."

So her father went on.

Why couldn't people understand? Gerhardina wondered. Still, they would know one of these days. She couldn't go on concealing it much longer. Already, it seemed that Lena van Heerden looked at her as if she knew. Yet it didn't matter. There was always a way out.

But on the road back to the farm Gerhardina admitted to herself that, when the time came, she would lack the courage to drink sheep-dip, like Sophie Lombard had done when she was with child.

The Night-dress

On 13 February 1931 The night-dress *was the second of Herman Bosman's Marico inspired stories to be published in Stephen Black's* Sjambok *under the heading* Life as revealed by fiction. *It appeared the same month as the first instalment of his second Schalk Lourens story* The rooinek *in the* Touleier.

Johanna Snyman stood in front of the kitchen table on which lay a pile of washing. It was ordinary farm clothing; her father's and brothers' blue jean shirts and trousers, her mother's and her own dresses and underwear.

Johanna took an iron off the stove, tilted it sideways and spat on it to see if it was hot. Then she went back to the table and commenced ironing.

It was a hot day in the Marico Bushveld. The heat from the sun and from the stove made the kitchen unbearable for Johanna's mother, who had gone to sit in front of the house with some sewing and a back number of the "Kerkbode." Johanna's mother was known all over the district as Tant Lettie. She was thin and sallow-looking and complained regularly about her health. There was something the matter with her which rooi laventel, wit dulsies and other Boer remedies could not cure.

On the other hand, Johanna was strong and robustly made. Now, with the heat of the kitchen there was a pink glow on her features. It was a flush that extended from her forehead right down to her neck and that part of her bosom which the blue print frock did not conceal. Her face was full and had just that tendency towards roundness that is much admired by the men of the Bushveld. But her nose was too small and too snub to remain attractive long after girlhood. And Johanna was twenty-three.

Tant Lettie, having put aside the "Kerkbode", began

embroidering a piece of cheap material that she had bought
from the Indian store at Ramoutsa. She was making herself
a night-dress. She held the partly-finished garment to the
light and examined it. She laughed softly. But it was not a
meaningless laugh. There was too much bitterness in it for
that. She wondered why she was taking all that trouble with
her night-dress, sewing bits of pink tape on it and working
French knots round the neck, for all the world as though she
was making it for her honeymoon.

She remembered the time she got married. Twenty-four
years ago. A long while beforehand she had made herself
clothes. That was on the Highveld, in the Potchefstroom
district. Her father had sold some oxen to the Jew trader and
had given her the money to buy things for her marriage.
That was a good time. She remembered that one night-dress
she made. It was very fine stuff that cost a riks-daler a yard.
She sewed on a lot of lace, and put in all kinds of tucks and
frills. When it was finished it was pretty. She ironed it out
and put it right at the bottom of the kist in her bedroom.
She didn't want any of her brothers or sisters to see that
night-dress, because they would make improper jokes about
it and she would feel uncomfortable. As it was, they already
had too much to say.

They went by Cape-cart to Potchefstroom for the wedding. Frans Snyman looked very happy. But he was excited
and she was afraid he would drop the ring, and that would
bring them bad luck. But he did not drop it, and yet they
seemed to have got bad luck all the same. When the
ceremony was over, Frans kissed her and said: "Now you
will always be my wife." She felt afraid when he said that.

That night they stayed at her father's house. Then she and
Frans left for the Government farm that Frans had bought
in the Marico Bushveld. She remembered the way she had
taken the nightdress out of the kist that evening after the
wedding, and how she had laughed at the frills in it, and the
ribbons and the lace, and had suddenly folded up the
garment against her breasts. But that was long ago.

She had kept the night-dress for many years. Often she looked at it and thought of the time when she had first worn it. But, somehow, it didn't seem the same. Each time she took it out it meant less to her than before. Afterwards she made a petticoat out of it for Johanna.

First Johanna was born. Then came, in turn, Willem and Adrian and Lourens. In the first year of their marriage there was a big drought, and it was only after half the stock had died that Frans decided to trek with the remainder of the stock to the Limpopo River. It was in the ox-wagon that Johanna was born. Tant Lettie remembered that she was alone nearly all that day, with only a Kaffir woman to attend to her. And Frans was in a bad temper because the Kaffirs had been negligent and had allowed some oxen to get lost. Frans was also angry because she had not given birth to a man-child. He swore about it, as though it was her fault.

Later on, when Willem was born, Frans seemed a little more satisfied. But it was only for a while. There were other things that he had to concern himself with. It had rained and he had to sow mealies all day as long as the ground remained wet. As for the two youngest children, Adrian and Lourens, Frans hardly noticed their coming.

Still, that was the way Frans was, and all men were like that. She knew he was sorry he had got married, and she didn't blame him for it. Only she thought that he need not always show it in such an open sort of way. For that matter, she was sorry also that she had got married. It would have been better if she had remained in her father's house. She knew she would have been unhappy there, and when her parents died she would have to go out and stay with somebody else. Or she might have been able to get work somewhere. But still, all that would have been much better than to get married. Now she had brought four children into the world who would lead the same kind of life that she had led.

Tant Lettie put down her sewing. Her face turned slightly

pale. Her hands dropped to her sides. She felt, coming on
once more, that pain which rooi laventel and wit dulsies
could not cure.

In the kitchen Johanna had at last finished with the
washing. Then she slipped quietly into her bedroom and
came back with a garment which she unfolded in a way that
had tenderness in it. She ran her fingers over the new linen,
with the lace and ribbons and frills. Then, having ironed it,
she took the night-dress to her bedroom and packed it away
carefully at the bottom of her kist.

The Man-eater

The man-eater *was the first of Bosman's post-prison Edgar Allan Poe influenced stories and the only Johannesburg story he wrote for the* Touleier. *In April 1931 it ran concurrently with* Veld fire *in the Bosman-Blignaut new critical weekly the* New L S D.

Unaware of Bosman's use of two names, a student of the short story, Reinhardt (Rip) Oberholster, was so impressed with The man-eater *that he spent over a decade trying to trace Herman Malan only to find him in the mid-forties as H. C. Bosman. Together they tried (unsuccessfully) to resuscitate the* Touleier, *and then to persuade Afrikaanse Pers Boekhandel to publish the collection of short stories now known as* Mafeking Road.

Although his regard for Poe led Bosman to speak of him as "a leak in the cosmic secret", The man-eater's *macabre theme and treatment must nevertheless strike readers as a startling departure from the sly, gentle humour they have come to expect from him.*

I couldn't help feeling that the man was mad, somehow. Especially the way his eyes flashed when he laughed. But also I couldn't help knowing that he was sane. Only it was a terrible kind of sanity. It was that dreadful sanity of the poet who finds himself a king amongst men, because he knows those dazzling words that a child knows, and that a grown man cannot understand. I mean the way in which a poet is sane when he clasps the stars and sweeps his hand across the firmament, and talks obscenely about the way the red sun sets in blood, feeling the passion of nature, unconscious of the psycho-sexual imagery.

Anyway, it is a strange story that he told me. If it is the truth, then it is God's truth. And if it is a lie, then it is God's lie, also, for it is a lie worthy of Him who invented the universe, and who first spoke about the leviathan. Or perhaps it is all just madness, this man I met on the Town Hall steps, and his story and the café in which we sat and talked.

For I know that in some things I am altogether mad.

It was early on a Sunday evening. The Salvation Army Band played between the Town Hall and the Post Office.

The band was playing red music. It is only now that the scientists in their pitiful way, adjusting their crude, steel instruments with faltering hands, are trying to establish the relationship between sound and colour—as if sound and colour were not exactly the same thing. What a hopeless lot of blundering fools these scientists are! They cut off a little bit of life—that trivial side that is material and is of no importance, anyway, because it is dead already—and with clumsy gauges and measures they try to find out what it is all about. The scientist's instrument—what could be more grotesquely inaccurate than the microscope? Then, when the scientist gets his dead results, he finds that they are all useless, and that the artist and the poet dreamt of them all thousands of years ago. This is the most pathetic situation in the universe, the puny scientist pitting his blundering instruments against the artist's dreams. Usually, the scientist is a hundred thousand years behind the poet. Sometimes, with an inspired mental leap, in which his instruments have no share, the scientist gets quite close to the poet—say within fifty thousand years of him. And all the time it is with things that don't matter to the artist. Those things which to the poet really are vital matters, the scientist never even begins to understand.

As I was saying, the Salvation Army played red music. It was a hymn tune. The words spoke of love and Jesus, but the sounds were of flames and blood and murder, and of that other kind of love that people do not know when they love only Jesus. But it is a love that Jesus knew. For Jesus was an artist. Pilate understood, and for that reason he called Him a king. Pilate understood that the penniless artist, with dust on his sandals and star-dust in his heart, was a king amongst men. This is the greatest thing that can ever be said for the Jews as a nation: they once had a king who was also an artist.

"Though your sins be as scarlet,
They shall be white as snow."

The men and women of the Army sang the words when
the band stopped. But they sang in a peculiar way, as
though they were not altogether happy about it, as though
vaguely they felt something in the music that was born of
the age-old lusts and rapine of the world. It was as though
they could not sing to their God in the manner that their
fathers of the dawn had done; they could not sing paradisia-
cal words to a red tune that told exultantly of rape. So they
sang that hymn as though they were afraid of its nakedness.
It is only children and grown men with minds like children's who are not afraid of nakedness, whether it is a
woman or a sunrise. Only the pure in heart can face
elemental things without putting a hand up to their eyes.

Red is for blood sacrifice and for hate and for love; yellow
is for the sullen kiss of a dying autumn; purple is for pain,
but it is an emperor's pain. And so it is with all music and
all colour and all words. But there is no purpose in my
going on to explain these things, because no-one will understand them but a poet, and a poet needs no explanations.

Anyway, it was there, on that Sunday evening, that I met
the man who told me this story. Perhaps it is a true story, as
the Odyssey and the Arabian Nights are true stories, or
perhaps it is merely a lie, as history is a lie. But you must
understand that the man I am going to tell you about now,
and the café we went into, and what happened there are all
things that I have invented. For a change, I have decided to
invent a story of my own. As a rule, I am indolent, and, like
Shakespeare, I am content to crib my plots from lesser men,
who have sweated over the medium of a good enough
theme, and then have not been able to make use of it, until a
man with genius came along and took their laboured contri-
vance away from them and infused into it the breath of a
wild and a gorgeous and a gigantic life. Sometimes it is a
monstrous life. But it is not the inert, pallid thing that the

mechanic constructs out of hammered words. Actually, I know of only two writers who are not mechanics. God be with them both. They need it.

"Look at that fat fool with the drum," a man said to me casually; "what does he know about the God he's thumping the drum for?"

I looked at the man who spoke to me thus. He was a medium-sized man with dark eyes that had fires in them; when he laughed there was madness in his eyes. I understood then that I had very much in common with him, and although our laughter was not similar, yet we laughed about similar things. That, of course, is much. It means that in the big things of life our reactions were the same, in the manner of the men of Sodom, all of whom experienced identical emotions when they learnt that there were two angels staying in their city.

"He's a pot-bellied Philistine," I responded. "He's a slave with a dirty soul. I wouldn't even be surprised if he's a devoted husband."

You know, you can tell these things about a man. For instance, there is that Johannesburg artist who can see as clearly as I can. I spoke to him only a few days ago. He got the sack from a local newspaper because he drew the editor as he is.

"Yes," the man with the dark eyes answered, "you're right, of course. I know that man. He's not a regular member of the Army. And he is a devoted husband. You know what that means? If there is anything apt to make a clean-minded woman commit indecent assault it is to have a devoted husband."

Here Le Roi spoke only half the truth. (He had told me that his name was Le Roi.) Whether they are in love or otherwise, no man and woman can live together for longer than six weeks without permanent injury to their spiritual qualities.

"The fat pig," I remarked. Why I said that I don't know.

" Do you like human beings?" my acquaintance asked.

"Not particularly," I said.

"I mean, do you like them to eat?" he explained.

"I don't know," I answered; "I have never eaten a man."

"Well, I have," Le Roi said. "And I'll never forget the taste. Your talking about a pig recalls that to mind. Human flesh, boiled with cabbage and potatoes, tastes like sweet pork. And that's how that fat drummer will taste. It would give me great satisfaction to eat part of him. Only, of course, it would make me sick. I had too much of it, that time. And you know that when you have had a surfeit of anything, the revulsion lasts for a long while. To you my slight prejudice may seem unreasonable, but nowadays nothing short of hunger could induce me to eat a human being. Like sweet pork——"

Le Roi spat on the pavement.

For a while we stood on the edge of the crowd. I had come there to study the superb technique employed by the woman whose duty it was to bring the collection up to three pounds sterling. It was a foregone conclusion that she would realise that sum. But it was thrilling to watch her moves. When there was another seventeen shillings to come, she cajoled her audience with sweet if faded phrases. At nine shillings she stormed at them. With five shillings short of the amount her voice was very low and soft; there was a note of restrained hopefulness in her utterances; there was the fever the canvasser feels with results in sight. The last half-crown took long to come. The woman turned round several times, shaking her right hand about. In her one-handed gesticulation there was an old symbolical significance that goes back to Ancient Egyptian priestcraft; but the woman did not know it and the crowd around her did not know it. Yet those are mystical elements that are common to all ages. In every religion there is something for which there is no word. And here was this woman, a carnal Christian and an unimaginative mendicant, performing that sacred gesticulative ritual that you find in the Egyptian Book of the Dead and amongst small boys.

The half-crown came.

A man threw it so that it splashed on to the pavement. I thought of Le Roi's spitting on to the pavement. The two actions seemed so much alike.

The woman flung back her head. She looked triumphant. With her chin up, for a moment the flabby wrinkles in her neck did not show. The crowd around the band felt with her in the consummation. She was tired, but there was a light in her eyes that came from the satisfaction of knowledge.

I glanced around me. A tall girl on the edge of the crowd encountered a man's eyes. She turned away her head, but her eyes turned also, so that they remained all the time on the eyes of that man, who for his part merely grinned and looked sheepish. Amongst the Nordic races of to-day those old lusts are dead, the clean lusts of our ancestors, who crossed the Rhine to plunge an iron sword into Rome's fluttering heart. In their swords lay the victors' strength; with that thrust into Rome's soft body there went also their virility. Only the women still retain to some extent that primitive heritage of the flesh. If you are observant, and you are able to feel things as well as see them, you can detect in a nun a host of vestigial mannerisms that were born of the awakenings of puberty. I never see a nun in a tram-car without realising that the mystical is merely another term that implies eroticism.

Anyway, Le Roi was a poet. But he wrote no poetry. In fact, I learnt later on that his only attempt at serious literature was a smutty limerick he once scratched on the wall of a public convenience. The point is that he lived his poetry, for it is only the real poet who can live his work. Those of us who commit our dreams to paper and canvas are a sorry lot.

"Well," Le Roi said when we moved off, "I ate a man once. There were three of us together. I won't tell you where. It wasn't as though we were out in the wilds somewhere, or in a desert. In fact, there was an Indian greengrocer just opposite, where we bought our vegetables. Three of us stayed in that room. Of the three one happened at the time to be dead. He had died of pneumonia, and that was regrettable, as we had entertained higher hopes for him. As he was one of our band, we felt that it was an inglorious thing for him to die merely because his temperature had gone up to one hundred and five degrees. That seemed so cheap a way of dying when there were in this world things like rat-poison and delirium tremens and rope. You see, in those days we were still ambitious.

"'Let us burn him on the water,' I said. 'We'll give him a Viking's funeral. That will help us to forget the pneumonia.'

"'No,' my friend replied: "we love him intimately. He has been more to us than a brother. For that matter, he has been more like a sister. It is in a strange way that we have loved him. Always we were one with him, like the pollen-laden wind is one with the rose it breathes on—like the ant-bear is one with the earth into which it burrows."

"'That's true,' I said. 'we have been one with him in life. Let us be one with him in death.'

"'Let us enter with him into the most complete union of which the flesh is capable,' my friend suggested. 'Let us eat him.'

"So we pickled this man whom we loved so much that we could not allow him to die, and with the vegetables we bought from that Indian store at the corner we made stew of him every day until there was no more left of him.

"He is dead, but he is with us still. He will always be with us. Where the two of us are gathered in his name, there is he in the midst of us. I shall never forget him. What is more, I shall never forget the taste of him. It was like sweet pork."

I walked down the street with this strange man who had the wild light in his eye. I envied him his experience. But what I envied about him even more was that sublime confidence which alone makes it possible for a man to tell a mad story that a sane fool calls a lie.

It was getting dark. There is so much that we can

understand about life when things get dark. But of the dark itself only God knows the meaning. Far off there still sounded the Army's Band music. Now and again, intermittently, we still heard the throbbing of the drum. There was the pulse of life in the throb of the drum.

"Yes," Le Roi said, "he's a devoted husband, that man with the drum whom we were talking about. I know him and I also know his wife. They keep a restaurant a few streets down. The woman is interesting. She had been married to an affectionate, slobbering Philistine for two years, and yet she remains fresh. Some women are like that. When I think of her I think of dew in the lily's cup. I think of milk in a yellow goblet and red wine on the ground. Her husband is kind and meek and considerate, and during all the while that they have been married he has not once kicked her in the ribs. Whenever he leaves for work in the morning he strokes her hair and kisses her. His caresses hurt her physically because they bruise her soul. To be embraced by a man with blood like dishwater."

We went into a restaurant.

"That is the woman," Le Roi said; "but she never looks at me in the way a woman looks at a man. She knows that I understand. What she doesn't understand is that when once you have loved a man so much as to eat him you can never again love a woman."

It was a small place in which we sat, but it was cosy. There was no one else in the restaurant but the tall, slender woman who took our order for a meal. Odd bits of straw and paper were scattered about the floor, so that I knew nobody would stop me from spitting beside my chair. I liked that café. There was even something about the cash counter that made me feel I could plank down my last shilling on it like a prince.

"She's got a child, too," Le Roi went on over the soup. "A six months old boy. And the child is exactly like his father in appearance. Which is damnable. But we can only see that the child looks like its father. The woman can see in the child, every day of her life, those thousands of little personal characteristics that go deeper than looks—all those things that her husband has got. Imagine how she hates the child."

The woman brought in the fish. For an instant I caught her eye. I saw then that Le Roi was mistaken. There was in her eyes a terrible thing that her face did not show. The hatred she felt for her husband was nothing compared with that other thing that was in her soul. It is always frightening to see a woman with a calm face and with eyes that have looked into hell.

"Two days ago she sent away the child to its grandmother," Le Roi went on. "So she says, anyway. I don't know. It's a queer thing to do to a six months old baby."

Once again I looked at that woman. She leant up against the counter with her left arm canted obliquely across her bosom. I have seen women stand just that way in great pictures. I suppose that is what they call an obsessional act. These habits of childhood persist to the grave, and if I told her what was the significance of her pose, only then would she understand. Obviously she was the only girl in a family of boys, and at that age when she found herself developing along different lines from her brothers the knowledge embarrassing to her, she concealed her shy breasts with her left arm canted obliquely across her bosom.

I forgot who ordered the stew.

After a few mouthfuls Le Roi dropped his knife and fork quickly. He looked at me with a white face.

"Let us go," he said hoarsely.

We left.

There is nothing more to be said, except that Le Roi reached the street a good distance ahead of me. In leaving he upset two chairs and a table that stood between himself and the door.

Veld Fire

Veld fire *appeared in April 1931 in one of the earliest issues of the new Bosman-Blignaut critical weekly the* New L S D *the initials signifying "life, sport and drama". A veld story, not narrated by Schalk Lourens, it ran concurrently with* The man-eater *in their literary monthly the* Touleier.

The co-existence of the inarticulate acceptance of disaster in the frontiersman story and the satanic symbolism of the city story was probably the first hint of a dichotomy that would baffle the Malan/Bosman-watchers of the 1930s.

I let go the pump handle and took off my hat.

It was very hot, and the sweat stood out on my forehead and ran down my cheeks. I looked across the laagte where my house stood in the cool of the kameeldoorns. I wanted all sorts of things, then. I wanted rain, so that the pans would be full, and there would be no more need for me to stand pumping water for the cattle all day long. I also wanted more cows and oxen; but then I remembered that if I had more cattle I would also have to pump more water for them. So I wasn't too sure. I even felt slightly pleased to think that in July the kafirs had stolen six of my Afrikander cows. It was funny to think of the way they would have to sweat, pumping water, for Afrikander cows can drink a lot.

The house seemed very pleasant. A kafir was chopping up a fallen trunk for fire-wood. That looked easier work to me than pumping water. Only the kafir was not doing it properly. He had only a chopper with a short handle, and he stood over the wood with his body bent double. Of course, the right way to chop wood when the handle is short like that is to sit down on the grass beside the wood-pile. When the handle is longer you can sit on a paraffin box. But only an ignorant Bechuana kafir would stand. Also, when you are nearly on the ground, you can nearly always rest your back against a big rock. That is why the Lord scattered so many iron-stone boulders right through the Marico Bush-veld. From what I know of farming today, I would never think of buying a farm without first making sure that it is full of large-sized stones.

I lit my pipe and then went on and started afresh with the pump-handle, but no matter how hard I tried, I couldn't think of an easy way of doing pumping.

"Kleinbooi," I shouted.

The kafir put down the chopper and came across to the pump.

"You pump water, Kleinbooi," I said. "You're no use at chopping wood. And don't leave here until the drinking-place is full."

I walked through the long grass towards the wood-pile. It was late in August and the grass was long and yellow and dry. In some spots it came almost up to my chest, and when I left the path to get to the wood I trampled a long swath of grass underfoot. It was eleven o'clock in the morning and in spite of the light wind blowing the heat was oppressive. I saw then that I couldn't possibly chop any of the wood before I had first gone into the house for a cup of coffee.

So I went round the house to the kitchen. I saw coffee which my wife had poured out for me, and while I smoked I thought of all that wood and of the pump-handle, with the knot in it near the end that blistered the inside of your hand, and of the way the sun burnt the back of your neck when you stooped down, and of how fine it was to be born a woman, when you had nothing to do except stand in front of a fire and wash dishes, and tell your husband you're sorry you married him.

"It's a bad job, pumping water for all that cattle," I said to my wife. "It gives me a pain just here, in the small of my back."

I drank another cup of coffee, after which I took up my hat and walked slowly to the kitchen door.

"God," I said, "Oh, God," . . . just like that. The kafir
Kleinbooi had left the pump. And the cattle had also gone.

For the whole of that part of the veld was one long sheet
of flame. The sparks from the tobacco I had struck out of
my pipe must have fallen on a blade of grass. Even as I
stood and watched the fire moved rapidly further. I called
the kafirs. But it was not necessary to call them. They had
all seen the fire, and knowing it was useless to try and fight
against it, had run away.

"We've got to save the house," I shouted.

One or two of the kafirs came to help me, but the rest of
them had hurried off to their own huts to stop the fire from
burning down their thatched roofs. Right down to the foot
of the koppies in front of my house the veld was in a blaze.
Koen van Rensburg, my nearest neighbour, had seen the fire
from the road along which he happened to be travelling to
Ramoutsa. He left his donkey-cart on the road and came
running down to help me. Between us we managed to get
the kafirs away from their own homes. Although they were
my kafirs, yet then they obeyed Koen more readily than
they did me. For when he got off the wagon he brought the
donkey-whip with him.

We hastened into the storeroom and emptied half a dozen
sacks of mealies on to the floor. The most we could hope to
do then was to save the house. Therefore I made the kafirs
take a sack each and light it at one end. I wanted to make a
fireguard round the house by burning a wide stretch of
grass over which the fire from the veld would not be able to
leap. We burnt a few feet of grass at a time, and then beat it
out again quickly, before it had time to spread, but the grass
was so dry and long that several times our own fire nearly
got out of hand. Still, we managed to make the fire-guard. I
worked alongside the kafirs, while Koen superintended with
the donkey-whip. When we had finished this task, so that
round the house there was a ten-yards breadth of blackened
grass, we noticed that all the kafir women with their children were gathered together at the back of my house. Their

huts had gone up in flames and they themselves had just managed to get away in time, with the exception of a blind and crippled woman of about ninety, whom they were probably glad to leave behind.

Then, also, for the first time we saw Koen van Rensburg's donkey-cart was gone. Terrified by the smoke and flames, the donkeys had stampeded with the cart. Fortunately, they had taken a safe direction. For now the fire could only spread one way, and that was towards the Bechuanaland Protectorate. On one side was the Dwarsberg Mountains; on the other side ran the government road, which all its length was very wide and grew wider every year, on account of the farmers always driving on the outside of it to avoid the pot-holes in the middle. Accordingly, the fire would not be able to cross the road.

With a fair wind behind them, the flames raced on through the bushes and long grass. They swept along, between the road and the hills over a breadth of more than seven miles. Koen and I caught a couple of horses which had been grazing on that part of the veld that lay below the pump, and we set off over the black and still smoking grass to follow the progress of the fire.

"Man, this is bad," Koen shouted, "All those farms in the Protectorate. Lucky. . . ."

He stopped talking, but I know he was going to say that he was glad his own farm lay behind us and could not be touched by the fire. And although he had helped me very much, yet I hated Koen for wanting to say that.

We rode fast, for horses are more tender in the hoof than donkeys, and, of their own accord, the two horses we were riding travelled as hard as they could go with the hot grass making things uncomfortable for them.

When we got near the fire we heard the roar of the flames eating up the grass, and as they caught the trees they crackled the dry twigs and leaves and branches. In a single flash a long red flame would spring from the grass to the top of a tall tree. You could see the whole tree wilt in one moment with its head wrapped in a huge sheet of fire, that roared and blazed with the wind behind it. In almost that same moment the tree would be burnt out, standing black and lifeless, its branches drooping straight downwards, like the coat-sleeves of an armless man.

Millions of sparks danced together in the wind. The smell of smoke made my nostrils smart. For seven miles that high wall of flame ran over the veld.

We came across numbers of dead spring-hares that had tried to break through the flames. I was glad that the cattle had more sense than to try to do that. The fire was travelling quickly, but as the wind had veered the cattle would be able to keep ahead quite easily, especially as they had a long start.

Koen and I rode on slowly after the fire. Near us something jumped out through the flames and fell on an ant-hill, a kicking bundle of burnt flesh. It was a duiker lamb. By the time it struck the ant-hill it had already stopped moaning. Koen jumped off his horse and looked at the lamb, but by the time he got there the animal had not only left off moaning; it was no longer kicking either. It looked as though it had been roasted in an oven. Nothing could pass through that fire and live.

"Poor thing," Koen said. He always had a soft heart that way.

It is strange how, in big matters, you can only think of one thing at a time. It is always like that, whether anthrax breaks out on your farm, or the lightning kills your cattle, or the wild-dogs are in your sheep-kraal, or you suddenly find out that the new minister is an agent for a company in his spare time, and is trying to insure you.

So it was with the fire. To-day I can hardly believe that then I was so short-sighted. All I was able to think of was saving the house. When I had done that I saw in which direction the wind was blowing, and I was satisfied that the cattle would be able to keep on ahead of the flames. Then suddenly I remembered.

"Koen," I said, "let us go home."

Koen looked at me in surprise.

"Why, what is the matter?" he asked.

"Nothing," I replied, "Only, after this I won't need to pump so much water."

Then we turned back home, riding very slowly.

You see, what I had forgotten, up to that moment was at the end of my farm there was a barbed wire fence, through which the cattle could not go. And as the fire was travelling then it would reach the fence in about half an hour.

Koen van Rensburg left me at my front door and went on alone to look for his donkey-cart.

That night my wife and I stood at the pump a long while and looked out towards the Bechuanaland Protectorate. It was a dark night. Far in the west there were faint crimson streaks against the sky-line, where the fire was dying on the hills.

Francina Malherbe

Francina Malherbe *was the first Schalk Lourens story to be published in a Bosman-Blignaut magazine other than their literary monthly, the* Touleier. *It appeared in May 1931 of their weekly critical paper* The New L S D *under the heading* Life as revealed by fiction *appropriated from Stephen Black's defunct* Sjambok *and ran concurrently with* The gramophone *(in the* Touleier*)*

After her father's death, Oom Schalk Lourens said, Francina Malherbe was left alone on the farm Maroelasdal. We all wondered then what she would do. She was close on to thirty and in the Bushveld, when a girl is not married by twenty-five, you can be quite certain that she won't get a man any more. Unless she has got money. And even then if she gets married at about thirty she is liable to be left afterwards with neither money nor husband. Look at what happened to Grieta Steyn.

But with Francina Malherbe it was different.

I remember Francina as a child. She was young when Flip first trekked into the Bushveld. There was an unlucky man for you. Just the year after he had settled on Maroelasdal the rinderpest broke out and killed off all his cattle. That was a bad time for all of us. But Flip Malherbe suffered most. Then, for the first time that anybody in the Marico District could remember, a pack of wolves came out of the Kalahari, driven into the Transvaal by the hunger. For in the Kalahari nearly all the game had died with the rinderpest. Maroelasdal was the nearest farm to the border, and in one night, as Flip told us, the wolves got into his kraal and tore the insides out of three hundred of his sheep. This was all the more remarkable, because Flip, to my knowledge, had never owned more than fifty sheep.

Then Flip Malherbe's wife died of the lung disease, and
shortly afterwards also his two younger sons who were
always delicate. That left only Francina, who was then
about fifteen. All those troubles turned Flip's head a little.
That year the Government voted money for the relief of
farmers who had suffered from the rinderpest, and Flip put
in a claim. He got paid quite a lot of money, but he spent
most of it in Zeerust on drink. Then Flip went to the school
teacher and asked him if the Government would not give
him compensation also because his wife and his sons had
died, but the teacher, who did not know that Flip had
become strange in the head, only laughed at him. Often
after that, Flip told us that he was sorry his wife and
children had died of the lung disease instead of the rinderpest, because otherwise he could have put in a claim for
them.

Francina left school and set to work looking after the
farm. With what was left out of the money Flip had got
from the Government, she bought a few head of cattle.
When the rains came she bought seed mealies and set the
kaffir squatters ploughing the vlakte. For three months in
the year, by law, the kaffirs have to work for the White man
on whose land they live. But you know what it is with
kaffirs. As soon as they saw that there was no man on the
farm who would look to it that they worked, the kaffirs
ploughed only a little every day for Flip and spent the rest
of the time in working for themselves. Francina spoke to
her father about it, but it was no good. Flip just sat in front
of the house all day smoking his pipe. In the end, Francina
wrote out all the trekpasses and made all the kaffirs clear off
the farm, except old Mosigo, who had always been a good
kaffir.

In those days, Francina was very pretty. She had dark
eyes with long lashes that curled down on her red cheeks
when her eyes were closed. I know, because I usually sat
near her in church, and during prayers I sometimes looked
sideways at her. That was sinful, but then I was not the only

one who did it. Whenever I opened my eyes slightly to look
at her, I saw that there were other men doing the same
thing. Once a young minister, who had just finished his
studies at Potchefstroom, came to preach to us, so that we
could appoint him as our predikant if we wished. But we
did not appoint him. The ouderlings and diakens in the
church council said that perhaps they could permit a minister to look underneath his lids while he was praying, but it
was only right that his eyes be shut all the time when he
pronounced the blessing.

For the next two years I don't know how Francina and
her father managed to make a living on the farm. But they
did it somehow. Also, after a while they got other kaffir
families to squat on the farm, and to help Mosigo on the
lands with the ploughing time. Once Flip left his place on
the front stoep and got into the mule-cart and drove to
Zeerust. After two days, the hotel proprietor sent him back
to the farm on an Indian trader's wagon. Flip had sold the
mules and cart and bought drink.

Shortly after that I saw Flip at the post office. The
dining-room of Hans Welman's house was the post office,
and we all went there to talk and fetch our letters. Flip came
in and shook hands with everybody in the way we all did,
and said good morning. Then he went up to Hans Welman
and held out his hand: Welman just looked Flip Malherbe
up and down and walked away. But with all his nonsense,
Flip was sane enough to know that he had been insulted.

"You go to hell, Hans Welman," he shouted.

Welman turned round at once.

"My house is the public post office," he said, "so I can't
throw you out. But I can say what I think of you. You treat
your daughter like a kaffir. You're a low, drunken mon-
grel."

We could see that Flip Malherbe was afraid, but he could
do nothing else after what the other man had said to him.
So he went up to Welman and hit him on the chest. Welman
just grabbed Flip quickly by the collar. Then he ran with

him to the door, spun him round and kicked him under the jacket.

"Filth," he said, when Flip fell in the dust.

We all felt that Hans Welman had no business to do that. After all, it was Flip's own affair as to how he treated his daughter.

After that we rarely saw Flip again. He hardly ever moved from his front stoep. At first young men still came to call on Francina. But later on they stopped coming, for she gave them no encouragement. She said she could not marry while her father was still alive as she had to look after him. That was usually enough for most young men. They had only to glance once at Flip, who of late had grown fat and hardy-looking, to be satisfied that it would still be many years before they could hope to get Francina. Accordingly, the young men stayed away.

By and by nobody went to the Malherbe's house. It was no use calling on Flip, because we all knew he was mad. Although, often, when I thought of it, it seemed to me that he was less insane than people believed. After all, it is not every man who can so arrange his affairs that he has nothing more to do except to sit down all day smoking and drinking coffee.

But although Francina never visited anybody, she always went regularly to church. Only, as the years passed, she became thinner and there were wrinkles under her eyes. Also, her cheeks were no longer red. And there are always enough fresh-looking girls in the Bushveld, without the young men having to trouble themselves overmuch about those who have grown old.

And so the years passed, as you read in the Book, summer and winter and seed-time and harvest. Then one day Flip Malherbe died. The only people at the funeral were the Bekkers, the Van Vuurens, my family and Hendrik Oberholzer, the ouderling who conducted the service. We saw Francina scatter dust over her father's face and then we left.

That was the time when we began to wonder what Francina would do. It was fifteen years since her mother had died, so that Francina was now thirty, and during those fifteen years she had worked hard and in a careful way, so that the farm Maroelasdal was all paid and there was plenty of sheep and cattle. But Francina just went on exactly the same as she had done when her father was still alive. Only, now the best years of a woman's life were behind her, and during all that time she had had nothing but work. We all felt sorry for her, the women-folk as well, but there was nothing we could do.

Francina came to church every Sunday, and that was about the only time we saw her. Yet both before and after the church she was always alone, and she seldom spoke to anybody. In her black mourning dress she began to look almost pretty again, but of what use was that at her age?

People who had trekked into the Marico District in the last four years and only knew her by sight said she must also be a little strange in the head, like her father was. They said it looked as though it was in the family. But we who saw her grow up knew better. We understood that it was her life that had made her lonely like that.

One day an insurance agent came through the Bushveld. He called at all the houses, Francina's also. It did not seem as if he was doing much business in the district, and yet every time he came back. And people noticed that it was always to Francina's house that the insurance agent went first. They talked about it.

But if Francina knew what was being said about her she never mentioned it to anybody, and she didn't try to act differently. Nevertheless, there came a Sunday when she missed going to church. At once everybody felt that what was being whispered about her was true. Especially when she did not come to church the next Sunday or the Sunday after. Of course, stories that are told in this way about women are always true. But there was one thing that they said that was a lie. They said that what the insurance agent wanted was Francina's farm and cattle. And they foretold that exactly the same thing would happen to Francina as had happened to Grieta Steyn: that in the end she would lose both her property and the man.

As I have told you, this last part of their stories did not come out in the way they had prophesied. If the insurance agent really had tried to get from her the farm and the cattle, nobody could say for sure. But what we did know was that he had gone back without them. He left quite suddenly, too, and he did not return any more.

And Francina never again came to church. Yes, it's funny that women could get like that. For I did not imagine that anything could ever come across Francina's life that would make her go away from her religion. But, of course, you can't tell.

Sometimes when I ride past Maroelasdal in the evening, on my way home, I wonder about these things. When I pass that point near the aardvark mound where the trees have been chopped down, and I see Francina in front of the house, I seem to remember her again as she was when she was fourteen. And if the sun is near to setting, and I see her playing with her child I sometimes wish somehow that it was not a bastard.

Karel Flysman

Karel Flysman, *an Oom Schalk Lourens story, was published in June 1931 in the only issue ever to appear of the* African Magazine *(formerly the* Touleier*). Commercially unviable, the* Touleier *was further inhibited by Bosman's abortive departure for London. (He got as far as Cape Town before turning back.)*

Karel Flysman was Bosman's first experiment with the socio-political "hensopper" theme to which he would return several times, developing and polishing it to the excellence of Mafeking road, *the title story of Bosman's first published collection.* Karel Flysman *bore no signature at all.*

It was after the English had taken Pretoria that I first met Karel Flysman, **Oom Schalk Lourens said.**

Karel was about twenty-five. He was a very tall, well-built young man with a red face and curly hair. He was good-looking, and while I was satisfied with what the good Lord had done for me, yet I felt sometimes that if only He had given me a body like what Karel Flysman had got, I would go to church oftener and put more in the collection plate.

When the big commandos broke up, we separated into small companies, so that the English would not be able to catch all the Republican forces at the same time. If we were few and scattered the English would have to look harder to find us in the dongas and bushes and *rante*. And the English, at the beginning, moved slowly. When their scouts saw us making coffee under the trees by the side of the spruit, where it was cool and pleasant, they turned back to the main army and told their general about us. The general would look through his field-glasses and nod his head a few times.

"Yes," he would say; "that is the enemy. I can see them

under those trees. There's that man with the long beard
eating out of a pot with his hands. Why doesn't he use a
knife and fork? I don't think he can be a gentleman. Bring
out the maps and we'll attack them."

Then the general and a few of his commandants would
get together and work it all out.

"This cross I put here will be those trees," the general
would say. "This crooked line I am drawing here is the
spruit, and this circle will stand for the pot that that man is
eating out of with his fingers. . . . No, that's no good,
now. They've moved the pot. Wonderful how crafty these
Boers are."

Anyway, they would work out the plans of our position
for half an hour, and at the end of that time they would find
out that they had got it all wrong. Because they had been
using a map of the Rustenburg District, and actually they
were half-way into the Marico. So by the time they had
everything ready to attack us, we had already moved off
and were making coffee under some other trees.

How do I know all these things? Well, I went right
through the Boer War, and I was only once caught. And
that was when our commandant, **Apie Terblanche**, led us
through the Bushveld by following some maps that he had
captured from the British. **But Apie Terblanche** never was
much use. **He couldn't even hang a Hottentot properly.**

As I was saying, Karel Flysman first joined up with our
commando when we were trekking through the Bushveld
north of the railway line from Mafeking to Barberton. It
seemed that he had got separated from his commando and
that he had been wandering about through the Bush for
some days before he came across us. He was mounted on a
big black horse and, as he rode well, even for a Boer, he was
certainly the finest-looking burgher I had seen for a long
time.

One afternoon, when we had been in the saddle since
before sunrise, and had also been riding hard the day before,
we off-saddled at the foot of a koppie, where the bush was

high and thick. We were very tired. A British column had
come across us near the Malopo River. The meeting was a
surprise for the British as well as for us. We fought for
about an hour, but the fire was so heavy that we had to
retreat, leaving behind us close on to a dozen men, including
the veld-cornet. Karel Flysman displayed great promptitude
and decision. As soon as the first shot was fired he jumped
off his horse and threw down his rifle; he crawled away
from the enemy on his hands and knees. He crawled very
quickly too. An hour later, when we had ourselves given up
resisting the English, we came across him in some long
grass about a mile away from where the fighting had been.
He was still crawling.

Karel Flysman's horse had remained with the rest of the
horses, and it was just by good luck that Karel was able to
get into the saddle and take to flight with us before the
English got too close. We were pursued for a considerable
distance. It didn't seem as though we would ever be able to
shake off the enemy. I suppose that the reason they followed
us so well was because that column could not have been in
charge of a general; their leader must have been only a
kaptein or a commandant, who probably did not understand
how to use a map.

It was towards the afternoon that we discovered that the
English were no longer hanging on to our rear. When we
dismounted in the thick bush at the foot of the koppie, it
was all we could do to unsaddle our horses. Then we lay
down on the grass and stretched out our limbs and turned
round to get comfortable, but we were so fatigued that it
was a long time before we could get into restful positions.

Even then we couldn't get to sleep. The commandant
called us together and selected a number of burghers who
were to form a committee to try Karel Flysman for running
away. There wasn't much to be said about it. Karel Flysman
was young, but at the same time he was old enough to
know better. An ordinary burgher has got no right to run
away from a fight at the head of the commando. It is the

general's place to run away first. As a member of this
committee I was at pains to point all this out to the prisoner.

We were seated in a circle on the grass. Karel Flysman
stood in the centre. He was bare-headed. His Mauser and
bandolier had been taken away from him. His trousers were
muddy and broken at the knees from the way in which he
had crawled that long distance through the grass. There was
also mud on his face. But in spite of all that, there was a
fine, manly look about him, and I am sure that others
besides myself felt sorry that Karel Flysman should be so
much of a coward.

We were sorry for him, in a way. We were also tired, so
that we didn't feel like getting up and doing any more
shooting. Accordingly we decided that if the commandant
warned him about it we would give him one more chance.

"You have heard what your fellow-burghers have
decided about you," the commandant said. "Let this be a
lesson to you. A burgher of the Republic who runs away
quickly may rise to be commandant. But a burgher of the
Republic must also know that there is a time to fight. And it
is better to be shot by the English than by your own people,
even though," the commandant added, "the English can't
shoot straight."

So we gave Karel Flysman back his rifle and bandolier,
and we went to sleep. We didn't even trouble to put out
guards round the camp. It would not have been any use
putting out pickets, for they would have been sure to fall
asleep, and if the English did come during the night they
would know of our whereabouts by falling over our
pickets.

As it happened, that night the English came.

The first thing I knew about it was when a man put his
foot on my face. He put it on heavily, too, and by the feel of
it I could tell that his veld-skoens were made of unusually
hard ox-hide. In those days, through always being on the
alert for the enemy, I was a light sleeper, and that man's
boot on my face woke me up without any difficulty. In the

darkness I swore at him and he cursed back at me, saying
something about the English. So we carried on for a few
moments; he spoke about the English; I spoke about my
face.

Then I heard the commandant's voice, shouting out
orders for us to stand at arms. I got my rifle and found my
way to a sloot where our men were gathering for the fight.
Up to that moment it had been too dark for me to disting-
uish anything that was more than a few feet away from me.
But just then the clouds drifted away, and the moon shone
down on us. It happened so quickly that for a brief while I
was almost afraid. Everything that had been black before
suddenly stood out pale and ghostly. The trees became
silver with dark shadows in them, and it was amongst these
shadows that we strove to see the English. Wherever a
branch rustled in the wind or a twig moved, we thought we
could see soldiers. Then somebody fired a shot. At once the
firing became general.

I had been in many fights before, so that there was
nothing new to me in the rattle of Mausers and Lee-
Metfords, and in the red spurts of flame that suddenly broke
out all round us. We could see little of the English. That
meant that they could see even less of us. All we had to aim
at were those spurts of flame. We realised quickly that it was
only an advance party of the English that we had up against
us; it was all rifle fire; the artillery would be coming along
behind the main body. What we had to do was to go on
shooting a little longer and then slip away before the rest of
the English came. Near me a man shouted that he was hit.
Many more were hit that night.

I bent down to put another cartridge-clip into my magazine, when I noticed a man lying flat in the sloot, with his
arms about his head. His gun lay on the grass in front of
him. By his dress and the size of his body I knew it was
Karel Flysman. I didn't know whether it was a bullet or
cowardice that had brought him down in that way. Therefore, to find out, I trod on his face. He shouted out

something about the English, whereupon (as he used the same words), I was satisfied that he was the man who had awakened me with his boot before the fight started. I put some more of my weight on to the foot that was on his face.

"Don't do that. Oh, don't," Karel Flysman shouted. "I am dying. Oh, I am sure I am dying. The English. . . ."

I stooped down and examined him. He was unwounded. All that was wrong with him was his spirit.

"God," I said; "why can't you try to be a man, Karel? If you've got to be shot nothing can stop the bullet, whether you are afraid or whether you're not. To see the way you're lying down there anybody would think that you are at least the commandant-general."

He blurted out a lot of things, but he spoke so rapidly and his lips trembled so much that I couldn't understand much of what he said. And I didn't want to understand him, either. I kicked him in the ribs and told him to take his rifle and fight, or I would shoot him as he lay. But of course all that was of no use. He was actually so afraid of the enemy that even if he knew for sure that I was going to shoot him he would just have lain down where he was and have waited for the bullet.

In the meantime the fire of the enemy had grown steadier, so that we knew that at any moment we could expect the order to retreat.

"In a few minutes you can get back to your old game of running," I shouted to Karel Flysman, but I don't think he heard much of what I said, on account of the continuous rattle of the rifles.

But he must have heard the word "running."

"I can't," he cried. "My legs are too weak. I am dying."

He went on like that some more. He also mentioned a girl's name. He repeated it several times. I think the name was **Francina**. He shouted out the name and cried out that he didn't want to die. Then a whistle blew, and shortly afterwards we got the order to prepare for the retreat.

I did my best to help Karel out of the sloot. The Englishmen would have laughed if they could have seen that struggle in the moonlight. But the affair didn't last too long. Karel suddenly collapsed back into the sloot and lay still. That time it was a bullet. Karel Flysman was dead.

Often after I have thought of Karel Flysman and of the way he died. I have also thought of that girl he spoke about. Perhaps she thinks of her lover as a hero who laid down his life for his country. And perhaps it is as well that she should think that.

Rita's Marriage

Rita's marriage *in July and August 1931 was the first of two stories by Herman Bosman to appear in that third Bosman-Blignaut periodical: their sporadically published and short-lived* New Sjambok *(after Stephen Black's* Sjambok).

Rita's marriage *was an attack on the family of the young woman with whom Bosman had consummated his first physical love affair, and who had inspired the erotic poems in his first volume of verse* The Blue Princess. *His preface was scorching: "Mostly these verses are about a princess to whom I gave millions of blue jewels that were real because I made them so. But I lost this princess. You see, she didn't want jewels: she wanted jewellery."*

A Jewess, she had betrayed his "jewelled firmament" by giving herself in marriage in the then customary fashion to a Jewish doctor. Rita's marriage *is so charged with venom that even the humour seems deadly.*

Rita was going to get married. Rita was tall and thin and walked with very short steps. People noticed the way she walked and speculated about it, idly, sometimes jestingly, until they got used to her gait, when they no longer found it peculiar. But with Stephen, the poet, it was different. He knew that the reason Rita walked with short steps was to induce other people and also herself to believe in the existence of a virginity which, years ago, she had lost on the Kalk Bay sands.

Rita hated sand. Even the white sand of the Johannesburg mine dumps filled her with hatred and fear and whenever anybody took her for a motor drive along the Main Reef Road she would close her eyes, blinding herself to everything around her until she got back home. In an upside down way, this was also the blindness that came to Paul on the Damascus Road.

A man who pretended to be a poet, but was only a poseur like Oscar Wilde, said that Rita walked with abbreviated steps because her ankles were chained; he said that her body was chained to convention while her free aspirations smashed themselves ceaselessly against the bars. Of course, this was a lie. And Stephen knew that it was not even a great lie. It was an ordinary psychologist's lie. Rita's peculiarities were of the body, and the body always goes deeper than any kind of aspirations. More especially is this true of a woman's body.

What was remarkable was that in walking with abbreviated steps Rita was merely adopting a custom of her ancestresses of the dawn, who wore light chains on their ankles to preserve their maidenhood. Rita, without understanding it, was trying to wear chains after she had been deflowered.

And this was something that only Stephen could see. Only a real poet could gather, from Rita's walk, the truth about the Kalk Bay sands. After all, this is only natural. A poet is there to make words. And in making his words he has to find places that they will fit into. Any burglar can tell that the man on the corner with the red moustache is a detective. A good burglar can tell that the man with the red moustache is a detective, even when he is disguised to look like a detective. But only a poet can tell that the detective on the street corner once dreamt of plum-blossoms in a garden.

Rita was going to get married.

It was a wealthy, unimaginative young man who had come several thousand miles from the Congo, that Rita had eventually decided to marry. Rita's mother had, of course, a share in the match, but the part she played was more of a negative character. It was not so much a matter of encouraging one particular unimaginative wealthy young man, as of discouraging others of the same kind. It was Rita's misfortune that she could attract only this one kind of man,

who can never bring to a woman anything more than a
warm, pasty kind of love. This is one of the things that a
woman has to endure with her body if she wants to be a
queen. Even the young man on the Kalk Bay sands had
been wealthy and unimaginative. For a long while afterwards, perversely enough, Rita regretted his want of ori-
ginality. It would have been a better seduction if the pro-
cedure had been less orthodox.

In the meantime there was the poet. He was in love with
Alice, who was Rita's younger sister. It happened at a most
inopportune moment, when the family was busy looking up
the addresses of 500 people whom they could invite to the
wedding with a reasonable expectation of getting wedding
presents. They had enough to do without having to settle
with a poet who, in addition to being penniless, was probably also hungry. Still, Rita's mother did what she could. She
threw a fit. She did it well, her collapse on to the settee
being rendered all the more spectacular by her bulk. She
was prepared to go on throwing fits like that, as long as the
settee held out.

But although he was debarred from seeing Alice, and
Alice was given a monthly allowance by her father on
condition that she cut out the poet, yet all this made no
difference to Stephen. He only wondered if he could not in
some way approach Alice's father with a view to getting
him to increase Alice's allowance. Because what Alice got
from her father wasn't enough to keep both herself and
Stephen.

You see, genuine poets are that way. They are stiffs and
vagabonds and they are unscrupulous. It wasn't that Stephen was immoral but he stood above immorality. All he
wanted that belonged to Alice was her soul, and that, of
course, was everything. Any man, if he is persistent though,
can usually succeed in getting possession of a woman's
body. And he'll keep her body until some other man, more
persistent than himself, comes along and takes it away from
him.

But only to the poet, who is both a king and a beggar, does God grant the sublime happiness of owning a woman's soul.

It is a divine privilege that comes but once in a lifetime, and then it is a ghostly barter, for in the exchange the poet also loses his own soul.

The preparations for the wedding went on apace.

Rita's nerves were unstrung. She knew what the unimaginative young man would discover on the wedding night, and she was also sure that the young man didn't know. There was some sort of inverted dramatic irony in the situation. The classic example of dramatic irony, I suppose, is when the Court Registrar has got the tip in advance that the jury is going to find the prisoner at the bar guilty of murder, and the prisoner at the bar doesn't know it yet, but still thinks he has a chance of getting off.

The situation is one that can furnish an intelligent Court Registrar with a profound spiritual happiness, and with amusement of a divinely instructive sort, during these long moments when the jury files into their seats and the foreman rises and clears his throat. The Court Registrar, with his inside knowledge, can derive intense enjoyment from a detailed study of the rapid and devastating changes of expression that come over the face of the man who is about to be condemned to death and still retains simple, childlike hopes that it mightn't be so, after all.

That was the position in which Rita found herself. She knew what the young man wouldn't know until after the marriage ritual. And yet, somehow, as far as she was concerned, something seemed to have gone wrong with the irony of the business. It brought Rita no happiness to possess this inside knowledge to which her wealthy and unimaginative lover had so far no access. Instead of experiencing elation through the power of knowledge, Rita was merely depressed. When they spoke about veils and orangeblossoms and bridesmaids—and presents—Rita felt still more depressed.

Actually, Rita lived through the days preceding her marriage in a state of tension known only to a pious man who has hurled a child out of a train-window because of the child's nagging persistence in eating oranges.

Then, around the corner, like a sanitary-cart playing havoc with a midnight romance of flowers, there lurked the poet. It is a pity that, with the advent of water-borne sewerage, the sanitary-cart, as an institution, is losing its hold on our imaginations. There is magic about what a sanitary-cart stands for; there is an appeal about it that we deliberately try to ignore, turning our faces the other way, so that we can talk more fulsomely about the majesty of empire. But the sanitary-cart is there. And only a great artist can recognise its presence and can tell simply of the power and poetry of the night and the mules and the buckets, of the drivers and the wheels.

The real test as to whether a man is an artist or whether he is merely sponging obscurely on the Temple of Art is to find out how he faces up to a sanitary-cart.

That wedding was the most fashionable affair.

It was the night before the wedding. The biggest one that had taken place in Parktown for a number of years. Five hundred guests assembled in a marquee in the garden after the flummery of the church ceremony.

They ate and drank until they had guzzled and swilled themselves full up to the neck. The bridesmaids looked charming and only one of them was natural enough to have sweat running down her face. But that bridesmaid was always in trouble, somehow. Long speeches were made and various forms of abandonment were indulged in that are characteristic of animals on heat in the mating season.

The wedding was a tremendous social success. This was only the night before the wedding, but we all know in advance what happens at that sort of marriage. It is over before the wedding morn. There is never a hitch. It is only at fairy weddings that hitches occur. The spells of the dew and the midnight trees and the warm stone with blood underneath it can weave their witchery only around the lives of elves and banshees and kobolds and princesses. The wedding of a princess's sister—who walks with short steps and wants to be a queen—comes off with the precision with which a tripe-dresser scrapes the excrement off the tripe. Pixies aren't sufficiently interested in a tripe-dresser to try and see what would happen if they make his hand shake.

Stephen was already married to Alice, and it had not been a flabby thing of organ-music and over-feeding and solemnity and fleshy lust and dowries. It was a ritual of bloodmarks on two brows and bleeding hands and curse on the green leaves. It is queer that people should go to the trouble of having themselves bound by empty social vows, when even a dud poet can break them with laughter that also holds passion.

A marriage made by a priest can be broken to leave nothing behind, except, maybe, the pain of a torn body, like piles. A poet's marriage can never be broken as long as there is grass.

Alice and Stephen.

Stephen had waited at night outside her house and had kept vigils. When there was light in her bedroom windows Stephen knew that Alice was there, awake. Sometimes she was there, asleep. Once or twice she had crept out in the night and had come to him, and Stephen, taking her hand, had led her away to the grass, where it was long and dark and the trees stood between the grass and the stars. It was a virgin love. Therefore, it was a hard, grey, flatbreasted love that had finality in it, like the sterile beauty of the Karoo, which no man can love, unless it is in complete nakedness. There is dark majesty in a sterile womb, which Isalah understood because he was a poet.

Where seed does not germinate is eternity.

Rita's love was different. It had to be. It was soft and flabby, like an amorous jellyfish. Like the full-green curves of the valleys around Table Mountain. A double-chinned, fat woman love. Rita and her young man—I have forgotten his name now, if I ever knew it, for I don't hate him and after love has died we remember only the names of people we hate.

Alice and Stephen.

Close your eyes, Alice and forget. The stars are thorns that pierce the torn grass. A little girl's hand is on the rough bark of the fir-tree; she looks at the sap glistening between her fingers and does not understand. There is agony in a flower-garden, the pain of two who have stayed beneath the moon together for a long while, and the man, holding the maid in his arms, dreams of a deserted white wall. Only those who have lingered long past midnight in the garden and have known this pain can understand the true significance of Christ's outspread arms and why the blood was mingled with water.

Anyway, it was the night before the wedding. Stephen loafed about the trees before Alice's house, which was a black house, because there was no light in the window. Stephen leant up against a tree, and as it was cold, he thought of the Equator and cursed the house because it was not white.

But it was only an empty curse and meant nothing. It was the kind of curse a man puts on his landlady when he calls her a whore for stealing his blanket, or when he calls her a cow for no other reason than just because she is a cow. A curse, to have power, must be put on with a kiss, Judas knew that. A curse is useless unless it bears with it the kiss of death. It is an invocation and a challenge. Slay, God. If not him, then me, God. But slay.

That night, in the same garden where the poet kept watch, Rita walked with the man she was to marry the following day.

Stephen thought of Alice, and knew that, although she was young, yet she was the autumn's princess. Perhaps for the reason that she was Stephen's princess, for Stephen was of the autumn, when she dies in a hard, still way, slowly, and lives only by what she has in her eyes. Consequently,

Stephen was supremely happy, as happy as only a man can be when he kneels in adoration before a god whom he has created with his own hands.

Rita paced about the garden, arm in arm with the young man. She was desperately eager to talk to him about her body, conveying to him certain facts about the Kalk Bay sands. She didn't quite know how.

"Sweetheart" she began, "will it . . . ."

The man put both arms round her, holding her passionately. She wasn't sure whether tenderness was the right touch. She closed her eyes. Then she bit her lips. Then Rita counted ten, and took a long breath and spoke all she could without breathing. "You know, I fell once accidentally when I was quite young on the sands at Kalk Bay, and Alice was there and she helped me up, and I was hurt, and you understand, don't you?"

The young man was a humorist after a heavy fashion.

"One of these frail, fallen girls," he said laughing. "The Salvation Army should have helped you up, not Alice."

"I . . . fell over a stone, accidentally," Rita explained, using unconsciously, as all women do at such moments the sexual imagery of the Old Testament.

"You understand what happened?" Rita inquired bravely.

This kind of discussion always roused the young man. To share with Rita in whispered words the secret intimacies of her flesh burnt his senses, like roasting raw meat on coals.

"I know, I know," he said, pressing her tightly against him and kissing her mouth and her eyes and as far down her neck as her frock allowed him. Then he released her.

"I understand," he said.

Rita looked at him swiftly. She did not speak to him again until long afterwards. She couldn't talk. There was a dryness in her throat. She could only feel that life was an ugly and a pitiful affair.

You see, a queen has to make sacrifices.

For in that one swift glance Rita saw that she had lost.

The man believed at that moment because he was pas-

sion-flushed. Later on, in their married years with the hot
lust in him, the fact that she did not come to him physically
intact would not matter. But in the chill of reaction he
would taunt her with his unbelief. He would talk sneeringly
and bitterly of what he believed to be the real nature of her
fall on the sands.

They walked through the shadows in that part of the
garden that lay nearest the street. Her lover's arms were still
close about her, and in Rita's heart there was a grey thing.

Quite near them there came the clatter of a cart, of heavy
wheels and mules' hoofs on the asphalt. The man tried to
hide his embarrassment under a pretence of being amused.
But he failed. He was that kind of man. He turned round
and propelled Rita swiftly in the direction of the house. The
advent of that vehicle of the night jarred him. It gave him
what was actually a guilty feeling, somehow, like a little
boy caught in an act of shame.

Rita hurried on with the man who would be her husband
after the daybreak. Her head was erect, as a queen's head
should be. Her steps were even shorter than usual.

Stephen remained for a long while under the trees, thinking of the wedding. For he knew that he was the bridegroom.

Heloise's Teeth

On 14 September 1941 Heloise's teeth *was Herman Bosman's second story to appear in the* New Sjambok. *It is the story of a man who is murdered in a lift. It so happens that shortly before, the uncle of Bosman's erstwhile love fell to his death down the lift shaft of a property of his still under construction, and which he was in the habit of visiting on Sundays when there were no workmen about. He had been the guardian of Bosman's* Blue Princess *and had forbidden her to see him.*

A macabre story, Heloise's teeth, *timed to appear when it did, was very likely an imaginative reconstruction with poetic licence designed to leave the bereaved family wondering.*

You won't really understand this story unless you are drunk. A god would understand this story, all right. A god putting his hand up to his eyes.

There is no such thing as prose and poetry and literature. There are only fairy stories and verses.

What attracted the young men to Heloise were her teeth. She had beautiful teeth—very white, with queer spots in them that gleamed in the sunshine. I don't mean her artificial teeth, either. I am talking about Heloise's own teeth, which the dentist pulled out the time they didn't know what was the matter with her.

Afterwards the dentist made her a set of artificial teeth, upper and lower, which she wore because she had to, but could never love. Heloise kept her own extracted teeth in a leather case.

Heloise was pretty, and the young men came to her and spoke about love, and told her that in her eyes were shadows like Boksburg Lake in the moonlight, and that in her hair was a fragrance that stirred them strangely, and that her lips held mysteries. Some of them even believed what they said about her, that Heloise knew that all the time what they were concerned about were the other and deeper mysteries, that were something like the spell of Circe. It made gods of men while they were still seeking, and when they had found it they were made swine.

Heloise knew this as all women know it, and as all men sometimes forget. But it is something that a poet never forgets, unless, sleeping too long for a while, for a while he dreams away his magic. When the old Christian seers and prophets murmured of divine mysteries they did not realise how near they were getting to the human body.

It was a curious business with Heloise and her teeth. When she was being courted by a young man whose feelings were as yet undecided she watched him steadily, and then at that moment when his emotions would become either passion or nothing at all she displayed her extracted teeth.

Other women in that position make a subtle show of their legs. Or they adopt a smiling posture that reveals the curve of their breasts. Or they become suddenly still in a deadly way, as a snake hesitating to strike because he is not quite sure of his poison.

That was the moment when Heloise, drawing the leather case from her handbag, scattered the contents on the table-cloth. It always worked.

There was young David.

"These are my teeth, David," Heloise said. "I had a lot of pain when they were drawn."

David reached forward eagerly. He was hers.

The delightful feeling of intimacy that came to him as he handled her teeth was bewildering. After all, teeth are ever so much more near and real than thighs that have only soft shapeliness—than breasts, that have only curve.

"This one must have hurt a lot when it came out," David said.

"Yes," she replied, "but don't you think it looks ugly, a tooth like that, with two such long roots?"

"Ugly," David repeated in amazement, "there is nothing about you that is not very beautiful. These two roots, and this hole here where your tooth was rotten—I have never seen anything lovelier in the Art Gallery."

In supreme moments even people like David talk poetry.

Without knowing it, David spoke in the language of Baudelaire, who first discovered the glory that is all in putrefaction—this startling grandeur of a king in decay. Beauty lives only when it has passed for always. Only that half-smile remains eternal that will not come again. If it does come again, later on, it is no longer a half-smile. It is a guffaw. It is the obscenity of a courtesan laughing about birth.

That is one reason why Byron could never be a poet: he did not know what Christ the Artist knew, that everlasting life can come only through death. Otherwise Byron would not have perpetrated the absurdity of imagining that if he were to see a girl again "after long years" he would greet her "in silence and tears". I or Keats would never have written that. It isn't poetry. It is only a romantic lie. And a romantic lie is almost as untrue as the heavy-footed rubbish turned out by that school of stable-attendants who call themselves realists.

David took Heloise in his arms and kissed her. Then their arms relaxed and they looked at one another. They knew that what was between them was more than just a handful of teeth. There was Andries.

I don't know why Andries has to be introduced into this story. But that's nothing. If I did know this wouldn't be a real story: it would no longer be art, like the fifty-third chapter of Isaiah or or Whistler's Little Girl in White.

Anyway, there was Andries. Andries was in a sense a cripple. It was a painful matter for him to walk at all. Little boys passing him in the street were in the habit of laughing at the ludicrous way he dragged his left leg behind him. But in the upper part of his body was enormous strength. Only very small boys would be able to detect the sublime humour of a cripple giant. This is true humour, whose basis is incongruity. There is nothing funny about a paralytic; a totally wrecked body cannot possibly excite laughter. A man looks funny only when he is partly maimed.

G. K. Chesterton, in spite of his pretence, never understood the real subtlety of children's laughter, which is identical with a genius's laughter. What was really humorous about Andries was the contrast between his huge chest and his massive shoulders . . . and his dragging left leg. But the children, when they laughed, always kept at least four paces away from Andries.

People said of Andries that he was the strongest man in the world. This was possibly true. But what advantage is it, after all, to be the strongest man in the world, if you can't run? A third-rate man can call you names, and you can't run after him and catch him.

David had called Andries names, often. David was childlike in many respects. It gave him a quaint and yet thrilling pleasure to throw taunts at Andries from the opposite side of the road, in the way that the other David had impudently thrown things at Goliath. Only, Andries wasn't killed by the words David threw at him.

There were nights when David would wake up with cold sweat on his forehead: that was when he had been dreaming that the giant had seized hold of him in the darkness. It was hideous. Yet there was also something delightful in a hair-raising contemplation of the horrors of being crushed and mangled in his savage fury. When David went to bed at night he locked the door very carefully. But when he saw Andries in daylight he jeered at him.

And of late Andries had been attentive to Heloise. I don't know how far they got. Maybe they had already reached the stage where Heloise showed her teeth. It has always seemed to me singular about a woman, that she can love a number of men at the same time. Perhaps it is because I have grown

to look beyond the things of love; perhaps it is that my eyes
have gazed too long past a woman in searching for the
goddess.

David and Heloise looked at one another in an almost
frightened way.

"Sister, there is blood upon the tooth," David said,
parodying a great poem. He laughed. Somehow, a parodist
always comes to a bad end. Which is well.

Heloise dropped her head forward, and Andries kissed the
back of her neck. It is singular how these things of the dawn
persist. Inferior lovers put forward the claim that they can
tell when a woman is in love with them by the light in her
eyes or the colour in her cheeks or the words on her lips.
This is all lies. When a civilised woman is in love with a
man she shows it, poetically and unconsciously, in the way
that the woman of the dawn showed it. She droops her head
forward, for the man to kiss her neck. By this act, the
ancient symbol of surrender, of passing under the yoke,
every woman proclaims her beloved as the lord and master
of her body. I am a poet. Therefore it is my business to
know these things. I am pleased to think that it is only
through my telling them about it that other people ever
know these things.

This is a tip to every father: if you come across your
daughter accidentally and she has a boy near her and her
head droops forward, then you know what has happened to
her. This is equally true of a school-girl who has just left
convent, and of a woman who has been a widow three
times. The old poetical things of the jungle cannot die.

When thoughtless fools say that poetry is out of date,
they don't realise that the only things that are actually near
to them and that have meaning for them are the things that
the poet tells them. And it is so easy to tell them lies. Only,
a poet never tells lies.

About two weeks after he had first found himself in love
with Heloise, David went down in the lift of the building in
which he worked. It was an automatic lift. On the third

floor two women got out. On the second floor a man got in. But David saw none of them. His thoughts were away with Heloise's teeth.

Suddenly David discovered that the lift had come to a stop, not on the ground floor, but right down in the basement. The semi-darkness of the place annoyed him. He stepped forward to press the button. The lift wouldn't move. David laughed. Then he became frightened. It was that mad, terrifying thing that psychologists call claustrophobia. He was afraid of the confined space.

Agitatedly David turned to the man standing behind him. . . .

David screamed.

Visitors to Platrand

*Visitors to Platrand, a Schalk Lourens story, was first published
on 1 November 1935 in the* South African Opinion, *under the
editorship of Bernard Sachs. Since early 1934 Bosman had been
living in London with his second wife Ella Manson. He had gone
to join John Webb, an expatriate South African colleague of the
Touleier days, who was to help launch his career as a Fleet Street
journalist. To fit his new image he abandoned his post-prison
pen-name Herman Malan and signed his work H. C. Bosman.*

Although they did produce a newspaper The Sunday Critic
*(from January to October 1936), but for one exceptional piece, a
review of T. S. Eliot's* Murder in the Cathedral, *his contribution
was uninspired in comparison to the pieces he was sending back to
the* South African Opinion.

When Koenrad Wium rode back to his farm at Platrand, in
the evening, with fever in his body and blood on his face
(Oom Schalk Lourens said), nobody could guess about the
sombre thing that was in his heart.

It was easy to guess about the fever, though. For, that
night, when he lay on his bed, and the moon shone in
through the window, Lettie Wium, his sister, had to shut
out the moonlight with a curtain, because of the way that
Koenrad kept on trying to rise from the bed in order to
blow out the moon.

Koenrad Wium had gone off with Frik Engelbrecht into
the Protectorate. They took with them rolls of tobacco and
strings of coloured beads, which they were going to barter
with the kafirs for cattle.

When he packed his last box of coloured beads on the
wagon, Koenrad Wium told me that he and Frik Engelbrecht expected to be away a long time. And I said I
suppose they would. That was after I had seen some of the
beads.

I knew, then, that Koenrad Wium and Frik Engelbrecht

would have to go into the furthest parts of the Protectorate, where only the more ignorant kind of kafirs are.

Koenrad was very enthusiastic when they set out. But I could see that Frik Engelbrecht was less keen. Frik was courting Koenrad's sister, Lettie. And Lettie's looks were not of the sort that would make a man regard a box of beads as a good enough excuse for departing on a long journey out of the Marico.

I felt that his chief reason for going was that he wanted to oblige his future brother-in-law. And this was quite a strange reason.

"The only trouble," Koenrad said, "is that when I get back I'll have to go and live in a bigger district than the Marico. Otherwise I won't have enough space for all my cattle to move about in. The Dwarsbergen take up too much room."

But Frik Engelbrecht did not laugh at Koenrad's joke. He only looked sullen.

And I remember what Lettie answered, when her brother asked her what she would like him to give her for a wedding present, when he had made all that money.

"I would like," Lettie said, after thinking for a few moments, "some beads."

It was singular, therefore, that when Koenrad came back it was without the cattle. And without Frik Engelbrecht. And without the beads.

And he said strange things with the fever on him. He was sick for a long while. And with wasted cheeks, and a hollow look about his eyes, and his forehead bandaged with a white rag, Koenrad Wium lay in bed and talked mad words in his delirium. Consequently, on the days that the lorry from Zeerust came to the post office, there was not the usual crowd of Bushveld farmers discussing the crops and politics. They did not come to the post office any more; they went, instead, to the farm house at Platrand, where they smoked and drank coffee in the bedroom and listened to Koenrad's babblings.

When the ouderling got to hear about these goings-on, he said it was very scandalous. He said it was a sad thing for the Dopper Church that some of its members could derive amusement from listening to the ravings of a delirious man. The ouderling had a keen sense of duty, and he was not content with merely reprimanding those of his neighbours whom he happened to meet casually. He went straight up to Koenrad's house in Platrand, right into the bedroom, where he found a lot of men sitting around the wall; they were smoking their pipes and occasionally winking at one another.

The ouderling remained there for several hours. He sat very stiffly on a chair near the bed. He glared a good deal at the farmers to show how much he despised them for being so low. And I noticed that the only time his arms were not folded tightly across his chest was when he had one hand up to his ear, owing to the habit that Koenrad had, sometimes, of mumbling. The ouderling was a bit deaf.

And all this time Lettie would pass in and out of the room, silently. She greeted us when we came, and brought us coffee, and said goodbye to us again when we left. But it was hard to gather just exactly what Lettie thought of the daily visits of ours. For she said so little. Just those cool words when we left. And those words, when we came, that we noticed were cooler.

In fact, during the whole period of Koenrad's illness, she spoke on only one other occasion. That was on the third day the ouderling called. And it was to me that she spoke, then.

"I think, Oom Schalk, it is bad for my brother," Lettie said "if you sit right on top of him, like that. If you can't hear too well what he is saying, you can bend your ear over with your hand, like the ouderling does."

It was hard to follow the drift of Koenrad's remarks. For he kept on bringing in things that he did as a boy. He spoke very much about his childhood days. He told us quite instructive things, too. For instance, we never knew, until

then, that Koenrad's father stole. Several times he spoke
about his father, and each time he ended up by saying, in a
thin sort of voice: "No, father, you must not steal so much.
It is not right." He would also say: "You may laugh, now
father. But one day you will not laugh."

It was on these occasions that we would look at one
another and wink. Sometimes Lettie would come into the
room while Koenrad was saying these things about their
father. But you could not tell by her face that she heard.
There was just that calm and distant look in her eyes.

But we listened most attentively when Koenrad spoke
about his trek into the Protectorate with Frik Engelbrecht.
He said awful things about thirst and sin and fever, and we
held our breath in fear that we should miss a word. It gave
me a queer sort of feeling, more than once, to be sitting in
that room of sickness, looking at a man with wasted cheeks,
whose cracked lips were mumbling dark words. And in the
midst of these frightening things he would suddenly talk
about little red flowers that lay on the grass. He spoke about
the foot of a hill where shadows were. He spoke as though
these flowers were the most dreadful part of the story.

It was always at this stage that the argument started
amongst the men sitting in the room.

Piet Snyman said it was all nonsense, the first time that
Koenrad mentioned the flowers. Piet said that he had never
seen any red flowers in the Protectorate, and he had been
there often.

Stephanus Naude agreed with him, and said that Koenrad
was just trying to be funny with us, now, and was wasting
our time. He said he didn't get up early every morning and
ride 16 miles to hear Koenrad Wium discuss flowers. Piet
Snyman sympathised with Stephanus Naude, and said that
he himself had almost as far to ride. "While Koenrad tells us
about himself and Engelbrecht, or about his father's dishonesty, we can listen to him," Piet added.

The ouderling held up his hand.

"Broeders," he said. "Let us not judge Koenrad Wium

too harshly. Maybe he already had the fever, then, when he thought he saw the red flowers."

Piet Snyman said that was all very well, but then why couldn't Koenrad tell us so straight out? "After all, we are his guests," Piet explained. "We sit here and drink his coffee, and then he tries to be funny."

There was much that was reasonable in what Piet Snyman said.

We said that Koenrad was not being honest with us, and that it looked as though he had inherited that dishonesty from his father. We said, further, that he wasn't grateful for the trouble we were taking over him. He seemed to forget that it didn't happen to just any sick person to have half the ablebodied men in the Marico watching at his bedside. Practically day and night, you could say. And sitting as near the bed as Lettie would allow us.

Gradually Koenrad began to get better.

But before that happened a kafir brought a message to us from the man in charge of the Drogevlei post office. The man wanted to know if we would like to have our letters re-addressed to Koenrad Wium's house at Platrand. We realised that it was a sarcastic message, and when we had pointed this out to the ouderling, he went to the back of the house and kicked the kafir for bringing it.

Koenrad's recovery was slow. But when he regained consciousness he did not talk much. Furthermore, he seemed to have no recollection of the things he had said in his days of delirium. He seemed to remember nothing of his mumblings about his boyhood, and about Engelbrecht and the Bechuanaland Protectorate. And although the ouderling questioned him, subtly, when Lettie was in the kitchen and the bedroom door was closed, there was not much that we could learn from his replies.

"Take your father, for instance," the ouderling said—and we looked significantly at one another—"Can you remember him in the old days, when you were living in the Cape?"

"Yes," Koenrad answered.

"And did they ever—I mean," the ouderling corrected himself. "Did your father ever go away from the house for, say, six months?"

"No," Koenrad replied.

"Twelve months, then?"

"No," Koenrad replied.

"Did you ever see him walking about?" the ouderling asked. "With a red handerkerchief over the lower part of his face?" We could see from this question, that the ouderling had more exciting ideas than we had about the sort of things that a thief does.

"No," Koenrad said again, looking surprised.

All Koenrad's replies were like that—unsatisfactory. Still, it wasn't the ouderling's fault. We knew that the ouderling had done his best. Piet Snyman's methods, however, were not the same as the ouderling's. His words were not so well thought out.

"You don't seem to remember much about your father—huh?" Piet Snyman said. "But what about all those small red flowers lying around on the grass?"

The change that came over Koenrad Wium's face at this question was astonishing. But he didn't answer. Instead, he drew the blanket over his head and lay very still. Piet Snyman was still trying to pull the blanket off his face again, when Lettie walked into the bedroom.

"Your brother has had a relapse," the ouderling said to Lettie.

Lettie looked at the ouderling without speaking. She picked up the quinine bottle and knelt at Koenrad's bedside.

Koenrad relapsed quite often after that, when Lettie was in the kitchen. He relapsed four times over questions that the ouderling asked him, and seven times over things that Piet Snyman wanted to know. It was noticeable that Koenrad's condition did not improve very fast.

Nevertheless, his periods of delirium grew fewer, and the number of his visitors dwindled. Towards the end only the ouderling and I were left. And we began discussing, cautiously, the mystery of Frik Engelbrecht's disappearance.

"It's funny about those red flowers on the grass," the ouderling said in a whisper, when Koenrad was asleep, "I wonder if he meant that there was blood on the grass?"

We also said that Lettie seemed to be acting strangely, and I said I wondered how she felt about the fact that her lover had not returned.

"Perhaps she has already got her eyes on some other man," the ouderling said, and he pushed out his chest, and stroked his breast. "Perhaps what she wants now is an older man, with more understanding. A man who has been married before."

The ouderling was a widower.

I thought he was talking very foolishly. For it was easy to see—from the look of patient dignity that passed over her face whenever she glanced at me—that Lettie preferred the kind of man that I was.

Then, one day, when Koenrad Wium was well enough to be able to move about the room, two men came for him. One wore a policeman's uniform. The other was in plain-clothes, and walked with a brisk step. And Lettie opened the door for them and led them into the bedroom very calmly, as though she had been expecting them.

Bushveld Romance

Bushveld Romance, another Schalk Lourens story, appeared on 17 April 1937 in the South African Opinion *under the editorship of Bernard Sachs. From his pen in exile Bosman contributed verse, essays and such well loved stories as* Veld maiden, In the withaak's shade, The music maker, Willem Prinsloo's peach brandy, *and others, many of which formed the basis of his first collection of short stories,* Mafeking Road.

Bosman's London period seems not so much to have provided him with the stimulus of a fresh environment, as to have confirmed his attachment to his old one.

It's a queer thing—Oom Schalk Lourens observed—how much trouble people will take to hide their weaknesses from the world. Often, of course, they aren't weaknesses at all; only the people who have these peculiarities don't know that. Another thing they don't know is that the world is aware all the time of these things that they imagine they are concealing. I remember a story my Grandfather used to tell of something that happened when he was a boy.

Of course, that was a long time ago. It was before the Great Trek. But it seems that even in those days there was trouble between the Boers and English. It had a lot to do with slaves. The English Government wanted to free the slaves, my grandfather said, and one man who was very prominent at the meetings that were held to protest against this was Gert van Tonder.

Now, Gert van Tonder was a very able man and a good speaker; he was at his best, too, when dealing with a subject that he knew nothing at all about. He always spoke very loudly then. You can see that he was a fine leader. So, when the slaves were freed and a manifesto was drawn up to be sent to the King of England, the farmers of Graaff-Reinet took it first to Gert van Tonder for his signature.

You can imagine how surprised everybody was when he refused to sign. They didn't know until long afterwards that it was because he couldn't write. He sat with the manifesto in front of him, and the pen in his hand, and said that he had changed his mind. He said that perhaps they were a bit hasty in writing to the King of England about so trivial a matter.

"Even though the slaves are free, now," he said, "it doesn't make any difference. Just let one of my slaves try to act as though he's a free slave, and I'll show him. That's all, just let him try"

The farmers told Gert van Tonder that he was quite right. It didn't really make any difference whether the slaves were free or whether they weren't. But they said that they knew that already. There were a lot of other grievances on the manifesto, they explained, and they were sending it to let the King of England know that unless the Boers got their wrongs redressed they would trek out of Cape Colony.

My grandfather used to say that everybody was still more surprised when Gert van Tonder put down the pen, very firmly, and told the farmers that they could trek right to the other end of Africa, for all he cared. He was quite satisfied with the way the King of England did things, Gert said, and there was a lot about English rule for which they had to be thankful. He said that when he was in Cape Town, some months back, at the Castle, he saw an English soldier leave his post to go and kick a coloured man; he said this gave him a respect for the English that he had never had before. He said that, for somebody who couldn't have been in the country very long, that soldier made an extraordinarily good job of assaulting a coloured person.

The upshot of it all was that, when the farmers of the Cape Colony trekked into the North, with their heavily laden wagons and their long spans of oxen and their guns, Gert van Tonder did not go with them. By that time he was saying that another thing they had to be thankful for was the British navy.

My grandfather often spoke about how small a thing it was that kept Gert van Tonder from being remembered in history as one of the leaders of the nation. And it was all just on account of that one weakness of his—of not wanting people to know that he couldn't read or write.

When I talk of people and their peculiarities it always makes me think of Stoffel Lemmer. He had a weakness that was altogether of a different sort. What was peculiar about Stoffel Lemmer was that if a girl or a woman so much as looked at him he was quite certain that she was in love with him. And what made it worse was that he never had the courage to go up and talk to the girl that he thought was making eyes at him.

Another queer thing about Stoffel Lemmer was that he was just as much in love with the girl as he imagined she was with him. There was that time when that new school teacher arrived from somewhere in the Cape. The school teacher we had before that had to leave because he was soft in the head. He was always talking about co-operation between parent and teacher, and he used to encourage the parents to call round at the school building just so that everybody could feel friendly.

At first nobody accepted the invitation: the farmers of Drogevlei were diffident about it, and suspicious. But afterwards one or two of them went, and then more of them, until in the end things got very disgraceful. That was when some of the parents, including Piet Terblans, who had never been to school in his life, started fighting in the classroom over what they should tell the teacher he had to do. Piet Terblans said he had his own ideas about how children should be taught, and he couldn't do his work properly if the other parents kept on interrupting him. He used to drive in to school with the children every morning in the donkey wagon and he took his lunch with him.

Then one day shortly after the inspector had called the teacher left. Because when the inspector walked into the classroom he found that the teacher wasn't there at all: he

had been pulled out into the passage by several of the
rougher parents, who were arguing with him about sums.
Instead, when the inspector entered the place, two of the
parents were busy drawing on the board with coloured
chalks, and Piet Terblans was sitting at the desk, looking
very solemn and pretending to write things in the register.

They all said that the teacher was quite well educated and
gentlemanly, but soft.

So this time the Education Department sent us a woman
school teacher. Stoffel Lemmer had been at the Post Office
when she arrived. He told me, talking rapidly, that her
name was Minnie Bonthuys, and that she had come up from
the Cape, and that she had large dark eyes, and that she was
in love with him.

"I was standing in the doorway," Stoffel Lemmer explained, "and so it wasn't easy for her to get into the
voorkamer. As you know, it is only a small door. She
stopped and looked at me without speaking. It was almost
as though she looked right through me. She looked me up
and down, from my head to my feet, I might say. And then
she held her chin up very high. And for that reason I knew
that she was in love with me. Every girl that's in love with
me looks at me like that. Then she went into the voorkamer
sideways, because I was standing in the door; and as she
passed she drew her skirts close about her. I expect she was
afraid that some of the dust that had got on her frock from
the motor lorry might shake off on to my khaki trousers.
She was very polite. And the first thing she said when she
got inside was that she had heard, in Zeerust, that the Groot
Marico is a very good district for pigs."

Stoffel Lemmer went on to say that Piet Terblans, who,
out of habit, had again brought his lunch with him, was also
there. He said that just before then Piet Terblans had been
very busy explaining to the others that he was going to
co-operate even more with the new school teacher than he
had done with the last one.

Nevertheless, when the new school teacher walked into

the Post Office—Stoffel Lemmer said—Piet Terblans didn't
mention anything to her about his ideas on education.
Stoffel Lemmer said he didn't know why. It appears that
Piet Terblans got as far as clearing his throat several times,
as though preparing to introduce himself and his plan to
Minnie Bonthuys. But after that he gave it up and ate his
lunch instead.

Later on, when I saw the new school teacher, I was able
to understand quite easily why Stoffel Lemmer had fallen in
love with her. I could also understand why Piet Terblans
didn't manage to interest her very much in the co-operation
scheme that had ended up with the previous teacher having
to leave the Bushveld. There was no doubt about Minnie
Bonthuys being very good-looking, with a lot of black hair
that was done up in ringlets. But she had a determined
mouth. And in her big dark eyes there was an expression
whose meaning was perfectly clear to me. I could see that
Minnie Bonthuys knew her own mind and that she was
very sure of herself.

As the days passed, Stoffel Lemmer's infatuation for the
young school teacher increased, and he came and spoke to
me about it, as was his custom whenever he fancied himself
in love with a girl. So I didn't take much notice of the
things he said. I had heard them all so often before.

"I saw her again this morning, Oom Schalk," he said to
me on one occasion. "I was passing the school room and I
was saying her name over to myself, softly. I know I'll
never have the courage to go up to her and tell her how
I—how I think about her. It's always like that with me,
Oom Schalk. I can never bring myself to the point of telling
a girl that I love her. Or even saying anything at all to her. I
get too frightened somehow. But I saw her this morning
Oom Schalk. I went and leant over the barbed wire fence,
and I saw her standing in front of the window looking out. I
saw her quite a while before she saw me, so that by the time
she turned her gaze towards me I was leaning more than
half-way over the barbed wire fence."

Stoffel Lemmer shook his head sadly.

"And I could see by that look in her eyes that she loved me, Oom Schalk," he went on, "and by the firm way that her mouth shut when she caught sight of me. In fact, I can hardly even say that she looked at me. It all happened so quickly. She just gave one glance in my direction and then slammed down the window. All girls who are in love with me do just that."

For some moments Stoffel Lemmer remained silent. He seemed to be thinking.

"I would have gone on standing there, Oom Schalk," he ended up in a far-away sort of voice. "Only I couldn't see her any more, because of the way that the sun was shining on the window panes. And I only noticed afterwards how much of the barbed wire had been sticking into me."

This is just one example of the sort of thing that Stoffel Lemmer would relate to me, sitting on my stoep. Mostly it was in the evening. And he would look out into the dusk and say that the shadows that lay on the thorn trees were in his heart also. As I have told you, I had so frequently heard him say exactly the same thing. About other girls.

And always he would end up in the same way—saying what a sorrowful thing it was that he would never be able to tell her how much he loved her. He also said how grateful he was to have somebody who could listen to his sad story with understanding. That one, too, I had heard before. Often.

What's that? Did he ever tell her? Well, I don't know. The last time I saw Stoffel Lemmer was in Zeerust. It was in front of the church, after the ceremony. And by the determined expression that Minnie still had on her face when the wedding guests threw rice and confetti over Stoffel and herself—no, I don't think he ever got up the courage to tell her.

Concertinas and Confetti

After Herman Bosman's return from England at the outbreak of World War II a precarious existence made him seek employment in areas related and unrelated to writing. He actually worked on a building site at the bottom of Twist Street before 1943 when a colleague recommended him for the post of editor of Pietersburg's bi-weekly United Party orientated newspaper The Zoutpansberg Review and Mining Journal. *Then in March 1944 Leon Feldberg, founder editor of the Jewish Times, resuscitated the* South African Opinion *with Bernard Sachs as editor and Herman Bosman as literary editor.* Concertinas and confetti *appeared in the April issue.*

Bosman had recently divorced his second wife Ella Manson on March 6 and, two weeks before the inception of the new South African Opinion, *married Helena Stegmann, a school teacher he had met in Pietersburg. Through Helena he overcame a bad case of writer's block and even began writing poetry again; but his attachment to Ella persisted until after her death in April the following year. Strangely, the idea of lost love haunted him in real life, as it did in literature, and was a recurring theme to which he would return many times in stories like* Concertinas and Confetti.

Hendrik Uys and I were boys together (Oom Schalk Lourens said). At school we were also class-mates. That is, if you can call it being class-mates, seeing that our relationship was that we sat together at the same desk, and that Hendrik Uys, who was three years older than I, used to sit almost on top of me so as to make it easier for him to copy off me. And whenever I got an answer wrong Hendrik Uys used to get very annoyed, because it meant that he also got caned for doing bad work, and after we got caned he always used to kick me after we got outside the school.

This will teach you to pay attention to the teacher when

he is talking," Hendrik Uys used to say to me when we were on our way home. "You ought to be ashamed of yourself, when your father is making all these sacrifices to keep you at school. You got two sums wrong and you made three mistakes in spelling to-day." And after that he would start kicking me.

And the strange thing is that what he said really made me feel sad, and I felt that in making mistakes in spelling and sums I was throwing away my opportunities, and when he spoke about my father's sacrifices to give me an education I felt that Hendrik Uys was a good son who had fine feelings towards his parents, and it never occurred to me at the time that in not doing any work of his own but just copying down everything I wrote—that in that respect Hendrik Uys was a lot more ungrateful than I was. In fact, it was only years later that it struck me that in carrying on in the way he was Hendrik Uys was displaying a most unpraiseworthy kind of contempt for his own parents' sacrifices.

And because he spoke so touchingly about my father I had a deep respect for Hendrik Uys. There were no limits to my admiration for him.

Yet afterwards, when I grew up, I found that real life amongst grown-up people was not so very different from what went on in that little schoolroom with the white-washed walls, and the wooden step that had been worn hollow by the passage of hundreds of little feet including the somewhat larger veldskoened feet of Hendrik Uys. And the delicate green of the rosyntjie bush that grew just to the side of the school-building within convenient reach of the penknife of the Hollander schoolmaster, who went out and cut a number of thick but supple canes every morning just after the Bible lesson, before the more strenuous work of the day started.

And I remember how always, after we had been caned for getting wrong answers, Hendrik Uys would walk down the road with me, rubbing the places where the rosyntjie-bush cane had fallen, and calling the schoolmaster a useless, fat-faced, squint-eyed Hollander. But shortly afterwards he would turn on me and upbraid me, and he would say he could not understand how I could have the heart, through my slothfulness, to bring such sorrow to the grey hairs of a poor schoolmaster who already had one foot in the grave.

And as if to emphasise this last statement about its being the schoolmaster's foot that was in the grave, Hendrik Uys would proceed, with each foot alternately, to kick me.

Yes, I suppose you could say that Hendrik was a school-friend of mine.

And once when my father asked him how we got on in school, Hendrik said that it was all right. Only there was rather a lot of copying going on. And he looked meaningly in my direction. Hendrik Uys was so convincing that it was impossible for me to try and tell my father the truth. Instead, I just kept silent and felt very much ashamed of myself. I suppose it is because of what the term "school-friend" implies that I am glad that our schooling did not last very long in those days.

If he had continued in that way after he had grown up, and had applied to practical life the knowledge of the world which he had acquired in the classroom there is no doubt that Hendrik Uys would have gone far. I feel sure that he would at least have got elected to the Volksraad.

But when he was a young man something happened to Hendrik Uys that changed him completely. He fell in love with Marie Snyman, and his whole life became different.

I don't think I have ever witnessed so amazing a change in any person as what came over Hendrik Uys in his late twenties when he first discovered that he was in love with Marie Snyman, a dark-haired girl with a low, soft voice and quiet eyes that never seemed to look at you, but that appeared to gaze inwards, always, as though she was look-ing at frail things. There was a disturbing sort of wisdom in her eyes, shadowy, something like the knowledge that the past has of a future that is made of dust.

"I can't understand how I could have been such a fool,"

Hendrik Uys said to us one day while we were drinking coffee in the dining room of the new post office. "To think that Marie Snyman was at school with me, and that I never saw her, even, if you know what I mean. She seemed just an ordinary girl to me, with thin legs and her hair in plaits. And she has been living here, in these parts, all these years, and it is only now that I have found her. I wasted all these years when the one woman in my life has been living here, right amongst us, all the time. It seems so foolish, I feel like kicking myself."

When Hendrik Uys spoke those last words about kicking, I moved uneasily on my chair for a moment. Although my schooldays were far in the past, there were still certain painful memories that lingered.

"But I must have been in love with her even then, without knowing it," Hendrik Uys went on, "Otherwise I wouldn't have remembered her plaits. Ordinary-looking plaits they seemed, too. Stringy."

"The postcart with the letters is late," Theunis Bekker said, yawning.

"And her thin legs," Hendrik Uys continued.

"Perhaps the postcart had trouble getting through the Groen River," Afrian Schoeman said, "I hear it has been raining in Zeerust."

"Maybe love is like that," Hendrik Uys went on "it's there a long time, but you don't always know it."

"The postcart may be stuck in the mud," Theunis Bekker said, yawning again, "the turf beyond Sephton's Nek is all thick, slimy mud when it rains."

"But her eyes weren't like that then, when she was at school," Hendrik Uys finished up lamely. "You know what her eyes are like—quiet, sort of."

His voice trailed off into silence.

And if a great change had come over Hendrik Uys when he fell in love with Marie Snyman, it was nothing compared with the way in which he changed after they were married. For up to that time Hendrik Uys had abundantly fulfilled the promise of his school-days. He had been appointed a diaken of the Dutch Reformed Church and he was a prominent committee member of the Farmers' Association and the part he was playing in politics was already of such a character as to make more than one person regard him as a prospective candidate for the Volksraad in a few years' time.

And then, I suppose, like every other Volksraad member, he would pay a vist to his old school some day, and he would talk to the teacher and the children and he would tell them that in that same classroom, where the teacher had been a kindly old Hollander, long since dead, the foundation of his public career had been laid. And that he had got into the Volksraad simply through having applied the sound knowledge which he had acquired in the school.

Which would no doubt have been true enough.

But after he had fallen in love with Marie Snyman, Hendrik Uys changed altogether. For one thing, he resigned his position as diaken of the Dutch Reformed Church. This was a shock to everybody, because it was a very honoured position, and many envied him for having received the appointment at so early an age. Then, when he explained the reason for his resignation, the farmers in the neighbourhood were still more shocked.

What Hendrik Uys said was that since he had found Marie Snyman he had been so altered by the purity of her love for him that from now on he wanted to do only honest things. He wanted to be worthy of her love, he said.

"And I used unfair means to get the appointment as diaken," Hendrik Uys explained. "I got it through having induced the predikant to use his influence on my behalf. I had made the predikant a present of two trek-oxen just at that time, when it was uncertain whether the appointment would go to me or to Hans van Tonder."

They were married in the church in Zeerust. Hendrik Uys and Marie Snyman, and that part of the wedding made us feel very uncomfortable, for it was obvious by the sneer that the predikant wore on his face throughout the religious ceremony that he had certain secret reservations about how he thought the marriage was going to turn out. It was obvious that the predikant had been told the reason for Hendrik's resignation as diaken.

But the reception afterwards made up for a lot of the unhappier features of the church ceremony. The guests were seated at long tables in the grounds of the hotel, and when one of the waiters shouted "Aan die Brand!" as a signal to the band-leader, and the strains of the concertina and the guitars swept across our hearts, thrillingly, like a sudden wind through the grass, and the bride and bridegroom entered, the bride wearing a white satin dress with a long train, and there was confetti in Marie's hair and on Hendrik's shoulders—oh, well it was all so very beautiful. And it seemed sad that life could not always be like that. It seemed a pity that life was not satisfied to let us always bear on our shoulders things only as light as confetti.

And as a kind of gesture to Hendrik, to let him sort of see that I was prepared to let schooldays be bygones, when the bride and bridegroom drove off on their honeymoon I was the one that flung the old veldskoen after them.

Afterwards, when I was inspanning to go back to the Bushveld, I saw the predikant. I was still thinking about life. By that time I was wondering why it was that we always had to carry in our hearts things that were so much heavier than concertina music borne on the wind. The predikant was talking to a number of Marico farmers grouped around him. And because that sneer was still on his face I could see that the predikant was talking about Hendrik Uys. So I walked nearer.

"He resigned as diaken because he said he bribed me with a couple of trek-oxen," I heard the predikant say. "I wonder what does he take me for? Does he think I am an Evangelist or an Apostolic pastor that I can be bribed with a couple of trek-oxen? And those beasts were as thin as cows. Man, they went for next to nothing on the Johannesburg market."

The men listening to the predikant nodded gravely.

This was the beginning of Hendrik Uys' unpopularity in the Marico bushveld. It wasn't that Hendrik and Marie were avoided by people, or anything like that: it was just that it came to be recognised that the two of them seemed to prefer to live alone as much as possible. And, of course, there was nothing unfriendly about it all. Only, it seemed strange to me that as long as Hendrik Uys had been cunning and active in pushing his own interests, without being much concerned as to whether the means he employed were right or wrong, he appeared to be generally liked. But when he started becoming honest and overscrupulous in his dealings with others, then it seemed that people did not have the same kind of affection for him.

I saw less and less of Hendrik and Marie as the years went by. They had a daughter whom they christened Annette. And after that they had no more children. Hendrik made one or two further attempts to get reappointed as a diaken. He also spoke vaguely of having political ambitions. But it was clear that his heart was no longer in public or social activities. And on those occasions on which I saw him he spoke mostly of his love for his wife, Marie. And he spoke much of how the years had not changed their love. And he said that his greatest desire in life was that his daughter, Annette, should grow up like her mother and make a loyal and gentle and loving wife to a man who would be worthy of her love.

I remembered how Hendrik had spoken about Marie, years before in the post-office, when they were first thinking of getting married. And I remembered how he spoke of that stillness that seemed to be so deep a part of her nature. And Hendrik's wife did not seem to change with the passage of the years. She always moved about the house very quietly, and when she spoke it was usually with downcast eyes, and whether she was working or sitting at rest on the riempies bench, what seemed to come all the time out of her whole personality was a strange and very deep kind of stillness. And the quiet that flowed out of her body did not appear to be like that calmness that comes to one after grief, that tranquillity of the spirit that follows on weeping, but it had in it more of the quality of that other stillness, like when at high noon the veld is still.

I knew that it was this quiet that Hendrik loved above all in his wife Marie, and when he spoke of his daughter Annette—and he spoke of her in such a way that it was clear that he was devoting his whole life to the vision of his daughter growing up to be exactly like her mother—I always knew what that quality was that he looked to find in his daughter, Annette. Even when he never mentioned it in actual words.

Annette grew up to be a very pretty girl, a lot like her mother in looks, and when it came to her turn to be married, it was to Koos de Bruyn, a wealthy farmer from Rustenburg. For her wedding in the church in Zeerust Annette wore the same wedding dress of white satin that her mother had worn twenty years before, and I was surprised to see how little the material had yellowed. It was pleasing to think that there were things that throughout those many years remained unchanged.

And when Annette came out of the church after the ceremony, leaning on her husband's arm, and there was confetti in her hair and on his shoulder I knew then that it was not only in respect of the white satin dress that there was a similarity between the marriage of Annette and that of her mother twenty years before. And I knew that that depth of stillness that Hendrik had loved in his wife would form a part of his daughter's nature, also. And of her life. And for ever. I saw just in a single moment what it was that would bring that stillness of the body and the spirit to Annette for the rest of her married life. And in that way I guessed what had caused it as well in the case of her mother, Marie, the wife of Hendrik. And I wondered whether Annette's husband would love that quality in her, also.

It was a very slight thing. And it was so very quick that

one would hardly have noticed it, even. It was just that something that came into her eyes—so apparently insignificant that it might have been no more than the trembling of an eyelash, almost—when Annette tripped out of the church, leaning on her husband's arm, and she glanced swiftly at a young man with broad shoulders whose very white face was half turned away.

The Story of Hester van Wyk

When Leon Feldberg revived the South African Opinion *with Herman Bosman as literary editor it was privileged to have among its contributors Sarah Gertrude Millin, Nadine Gordimer, Doris Lessing, Alan Paton, Uys Krige, Nicholas Monsarrat, Gordon Vorster and Lionel Abrahams. Herman Bosman contributed short stories, essays, literary and art criticism and reprinted some of his earlier poetry, saving "work in progress" for reasons best known to himself. He also personally pounded the pavements to sell enough advertising space to help keep it going. The story of Hester van Wyk appeared in its fourth issue.*

When I think of the story of Hester van Wyk I often wonder what is it about some stories that I have wanted to tell (Oom Schalk Lourens said). About things that have happened and about people that I have known—and that I still know, some of them: if you can call it knowing a person when your mule-carts pass each other on the Government road, and you wave your hat cheerfully and call out that it will be a good season for the crops, if only the stalk-borers and other pests keep away, and the other person just nods at you, with a distant sort of look in his eyes, and says, yes, the Marico Bushveld has unfortunately got more than one kind of pest.

That was what Gawie Steyn said to me one afternoon on the Government road, when I was on my way to the Droedal post office for letters and he was on his way home. And it was because of the sorrowful sort of way in which he uttered the word "unfortunately" that I knew that Gawie Steyn had heard what I had said about him to Frik Prinsloo three weeks before, after the meeting of the Dwarsberg debating society in the schoolroom next to the poort.

In any case, I never finished that story that I told Frik Prinsloo about Gawie Steyn, although I began telling it

colourfully enough that night after the meeting of the
debating society was over and the farmers and their wives
and children had all gone home, and Frik Prinsloo and I
were sitting alone on two desks in the middle of the
school-room, with our feet up, and our pipes pleasantly
filled with strong plug-cut tobacco whose thick blue fumes
made the school-teacher cough violently at intervals.

The school-master was seated at his table, with his head
in his hands, and his face looking very pale in the light of
the one paraffin lamp. And he was waiting for us to leave so
that he could blow out his lamp and lock up the school-
room and go home.

The school-master did not interrupt us only with his
coughing but also in other ways. For instance, he told us on
several occasions that he had a weak chest, and if we had
made up our minds to stay on like this in the class-room,
talking, after the meeting was over, would we mind very
much, he asked, if he opened one of the windows to let out
some of the blue clouds of tobacco smoke.

But Frik Prinsloo said that we would mind very much.
Not for our sakes, Frik said, but for the school-master's
sake. There was nothing worse, Frik explained, than for a
man with a weak chest to sit in a room with a window
open.

"It is nothing for us," Frik Prinsloo said, "for Schalk
Lourens and myself to sit in a room with an open window.
We are two Bushveld farmers with sturdy physiques who
have been through the Boer War and through the anthrax
pestilence. We have survived not only human hardships, but
also cattle and sheep and pig diseases. At Magersfontein I
even slept in an aardvark hole that was half-full of water
with a piece of newspaper tied around my left ankle for the
rheumatism. And even so neither Schalk Lourens nor I will
be so foolish as to be in a room that has got a window
open."

"No," I agreed. "Never."

"And you have to take greater care of your health than

any of us," Frik Prinsloo said to the school-teacher. "With
your weak chest it would be dangerous for you to have a
window open in here. Why, you can't even stand our
tobacco smoke. Look at the way you are coughing right
now."

After he had knocked the ash out of his pipe into an
inkwell that was let into a little round hole in one of the
desks, an action which he had performed just in order to
show how familiar, for an uneducated man, he was with the
ways of a school-room, Frik started telling the school-
teacher about other places he had slept in, both during the
Boer War and at another time when he was doing transport
driving.

Frik Prinsloo embarked on a description of the hardships
of a transport driver's life in the old days. It was a story that
seemed longer than the most ambitious journey ever undertaken by ox-wagon, and much heavier, and more round-
about. And there was one place where Frik Prinsloo's story
got stuck much more hopelessly than any of his ox-wagons
had ever got stuck in a drift.

Then the school-master said, please, gentlemen, he could
not stand it any more. His health was bad, and while he
could perhaps arrange to let us have the use of the
schoolroom on some other night, so that I could finish the
story that I appeared to be telling to Mr. Prinsloo, and he
would even provide the paraffin for the lamp himself, he
really had to go home and get some sleep.

But Frik Prinsloo said the school-master did not need to
worry about the paraffin. We could sit just as comfortably
in the dark and talk, he said. For that matter, the school-
master could go to sleep in the class-room, if he liked. Just
like that, sitting at the table.

"You already look half asleep," Fritz told him, winking at
me, "and sleeping in a school-room is a lot better than what
happened to me during the English advance on Bloemfontein, when I slept in a donga with a lot of slime and mud
and slippery tadpoles at the bottom.

"In a donga half-full of water with a piece of mealie-sacking fastened around your stomach because of the colic," the school-teacher said, speaking with his head still between his hands. "And for heaven's sake, if you have got to sleep out on the veld, why don't you sleep on top of it? Why must you go and lie inside a hole full of water or inside a slimy donga? If you farmers have had hard lives, it seems to me that you yourselves did quite a lot to make them like that."

We ignored this remark of the school-master's which we both realised was based on his lack of worldly experience, and I went on to relate to Frik Prinsloo those incidents from the life of Gawie Steyn that were responsible for Gawie's talking about Marico pests, some weeks later, in gloomy tones, on the road winding between the thorn trees to the post office.

And this was one of those stories that I never finished. Because the school-master fell asleep at his table, with the result that he didn't cough any more, and I could see that because of this Frik Prinsloo could not derive the same amount of amusement from my story. And what is even more strange is that I also found that the funny parts in the story did not sound so funny any more, now that the school-master was no longer in discomfort. The story seemed to have had much more life in it, somehow, in the earlier stages, when the school-master was anxiously waiting for us to go home, and coughing at intervals through the blue haze of our tobacco smoke.

"And so that man came round again the next night and sang some more songs to Gawie Steyn's wife," I said, "and they were old songs that he sang."

"It sounds to me as though he is even snoring," Frik Prinsloo said. "Imagine that for ill-bred. Here are you telling a story that teaches one all about the true and deep things of life and the school-master is lying with his head on the table, snoring."

"And when Gawie Steyn started objecting after a while,"

I continued, with a certain amount of difficulty, "the man said the excuse he had to offer was that they were all old songs, anyway, and they didn't mean very much. Old songs had no meaning. They were only dead things from the past. They were yellowed and dust-laden, the man said."

"I've got a good mind to wake him," Frik Prinsloo went on. "First he disturbs us with his coughing and now I can't hear what you're saying because of his snoring. It will be a good thing if we just go home and leave him. He seems so attached to his school-room. Even staying behind at night to sleep in it. What would people say if I liked ploughing so much that I didn't go home at night, but just lay down and slept on a strip of grass next to a furrow?"

"Then Gawie Steyn said to this man," I continued, with greater difficulty than ever before, "he said that it wasn't so much the old songs he objected to. The old songs might be well enough. But the way his wife listened to the songs, he said, seemed to him to be not so much like an old song as like an old story."

"Not that I don't sleep out on the lands sometimes," Frik Prinsloo explained, "and even in the ploughing season. But then it is in the early afternoon of a hot day. And the kaffirs go on with the ploughing all the same. And it is very refreshing then, to sleep under a withaak tree knowing that the kaffirs are at work in the sun. Sleeping on a strip of green grass next to a furrow . . ."

"Or inside the furrow," the school-master said, and we only noticed then that he was no longer snoring. "Inside a furrow half-filled with wet fertilizer and with a turnip fastened on your head because of the blue tongue."

As I have said, this story about Gawie Steyn and his wife is one of those stories that I never finished telling. And I would never have known, either, that Frik Prinsloo had listened to as much of it as I had told him, if it wasn't for Gawie Steyn's manner of greeting me on the Government road, three weeks later, with sorrowful politeness, like an Englishman.

There is always something unusual about a story that does not come to an end on its own. It is as though that story keeps going on, getting told in a different way each time, as though the story itself is trying to find out what happened next.

It was like the way life came to Hester van Wyk.

Hester was a very pretty girl, with black hair and a way of smiling that seemed very childlike, until you were close enough to her to see what was in her eyes, and then you realised, in that same moment, that no child had ever smiled like that. And whether it was for her black hair or whether it was because of her smile, it so happened that Hester van Wyk was hardly ever without a lover. They came to her, the young men from the neighbourhood. But they also went away again. They tarried for a while, like birds in their passage, and they paid court to her, and sometimes the period in which they wooed her was quite long, and at other times again she would have a lover whose ardour seemed to last for no longer than a few brief weeks before he also went his way.

And it seemed that the story of Hester van Wyk and her lovers was also one of those stories that I have mentioned to you, whose end never gets told.

And Gert van Wyk, Hester's father, would talk to me about these young men that came into his daughter's life. He talked to me both as a neighbour and as a relative on his wife's side, and while what he said to me about Hester and her lovers were mostly words spoken lightly, in the way that you flick a pebble into a dam, and watch the yellow ripples widening, there were also times when he spoke differently. And then what he said was like the way a footsore wanderer flings his pack on to the ground. to the ground.

"She's a pretty girl," Gert said to me. "Yes, she is pretty enough. But her trouble is that she is too soft-hearted. These young men come to her, and they tell her stories. Sad stories about their lives. And she listens to their stories. And she feels sorry for them. And she says that they must be very nice young men for life to have treated them so badly. She even tries to tell me some of these stories, so that I should also feel sorry for them. But, of course, I have got too much sense to listen. I simply tell her—"

"Yes," I answered, nodding, "you tell her that what the young man says is a lot of lies. And by the time you have convinced her about one lover's lies you find that he has already departed, and that some other young man has got into the habit of coming to your house three times a week, and that he is busy telling her a totally new and different story."

"That's what he imagines," Gert van Wyk replies, "that it's new. But it's always the same old story. Only, instead of telling of his unhappy childhood the new young man will talk about his aged mother, or about how life has been cruel to him, so that he has got to help on the farm, for which he isn't suited at all, because it makes him dizzy to have to pump water out of the borehole for the cattle—up and down, up and down, like that, with the pump-handle—when all the time his real ambition is to have the job of wearing a blue and gold uniform outside of a bioscope in Johannesburg. And my daughter Hester is so soft-hearted that she goes on listening to these same stupid stories day after day, year in and year out."

"Yes," I said, "they are the same old stories."

And I thought of what Gawie Steyn said about the man who sang old songs to his wife. And it seemed that Hester van Wyk's was also an old story, and that for that reason it would never end.

"Did she also have a young man who said that he was not worthy of her because he was not educated?" I asked Gert. "And did she take pity on him because he said people looked down on him because of his table manners?"

"Yes," Gert answered with alacrity, "he said he was badly brought up and always forgot to take the teaspoon out of the cup before drinking his coffee."

"Did she also have a young man who got her sympathy by telling her that he had fallen in love years ago, and that he had lost that girl, because her parents had objected to him, and that he could never fall in love again?"

"Quite right," Gert said, "this young man said that his first girl's parent refused to let her marry him because his forehead was too low. Even though he tried to make it look higher by training his eyebrows down and shaving the hair off most of the top of his head. But how do you know all these things?"

"There are only a few stories that young men tell girls in order to get their sympathy," I said to Gert. "There are only a handful of stories like that. But it seems to me that your daughter Hester has been told them all. And more than once, too, sometimes, by the look of it."

"And you can imagine how awful that young man with the low forehead looked," Gert continued. "He must have been unattractive enough before. But with his eyebrows trained down and the top of his head shaved clean off, he looked more like a—"

"And for that very reason, of course," I explained, "your daughter Hester fell in love with him. After she had heard his story."

And it seemed to me that the oldest story of all must be the story of a woman's heart.

It was some years after this, when Gert van Wyk and his family had moved out of the Marico into the Waterberg, that I heard that Hester van Wyk had married. And I knew then what had happened, of course. And I knew it even without Gert having had to tell me.

I knew then that some young man must have come to Hester van Wyk from out of some far-lying part of the Waterberg. He came to her and found her. And in finding her he had no story to tell.

But what I have no means of telling, now that I have related to you all that I know, is whether this is the end of the story about Hester van Wyk.

Campfires at Nagmaal

By June 1945 when Campfires at Nagmaal *appeared, the* South African Opinion *of the forties had been going for fifteen months; and Bosman's second wife Ella Manson, whom he could never abandon permanently, had been dead for three. Although* Campfires at Nagmaal *proceeds gently at the pace of the ox, there appeared, also in the* Opinion *in the June and July issues two essays on cities and dorps respectively. They were motifs that preoccupied his first novel* Jacaranda in the Night. *In the same issue as* Campfires at Nagmaal *he wrote: "The difference between the city and the farm is, alas, age-old. The city has gutters."*

Of course, the old days, were best (Oom Schalk Lourens said), I mean the really old days. Those times when we still used to pray, "Lord give us food and clothes. The veldskoens we make ourselves."

There was faith in the land in those days. And when things went wrong we used to rely on our own hands and wills, and when we asked for the help of the Lord we also knew the strength of our trek-chains. It was quite a few years before the Boer War that what I can call the old days came to an end. That was when the Boers in these parts stopped making the soles of their veldskoens out of strips of raw leather that they cut from quagga skins. Instead, they started using the new kind of blue sole that came up from the Cape in big square pieces, and that they bought at the Indian store.

I remember the first time I made myself a pair of veldskoens out of that blue sole. The stuff was easy to work with, and smooth. And all the time I was making the veldskoens I knew it was very wrong. And I was still more disappointed when I found that the blue sole wore well. If anything, it was even better than raw quagga hide. This circumstance was very regrettable to me. And there remained something foreign to me about those veldskoens, even after they had served me through two Kaffir wars.

It was in the early days, also, that a strange set of circumstances unfolded, in which the lives of three people. Maans Prinsloo and Stoffelina Lemmer and Petrus Steyn, became intertwined like the strands of the grass covers that native women weave for their beer-pots: in some places your eye can separate the various strands of plaited grass, the one from the other; in other places the weaving is all of one piece.

And the story of the lives of these three people, two men and a girl, is something that could only have happened long ago, when there was still faith in the Transvaal, and the stars in the sky were constant, and only the wind changed.

Maans Prinsloo and I were young men together, and I knew Stoffelina Lemmer well, also. But because Petrus Steyn, who was a few years older than we were, lived some distance away, to the north, on the borders of the Bechuanaland Protectorate, I did not see him very often. We met mostly at Nagmaals, and then Petrus Steyn would recount to us, at great length, the things he had seen and the events that had befallen him on his periodical treks into the further parts of the Kalahari desert.

You can imagine that these stories of Petrus Steyn's were very tedious to listen to. They were empty as the desert is, and as unending. And as flat.

After all, it is easy to understand that Petrus Steyn's visits to the Kalahari desert would not give him very much to talk about that would be of interest to the listener—no matter how far he trekked. Simply because a desert is a desert. One part of it is exactly like another part. Thousands of square miles of sand dotted with occasional thorn-trees. And a stray buck or two. And, now and again, a few Bushmen who have also strayed—but who don't know it, of course.

I have noticed that Bushmen are always in a hurry. But they have nowhere to go to. Where they are running to is all just desert, like where they came from. So they never know where they are, either. But because they don't care where they are it doesn't matter to them that they are lost. They just don't know any better. All they are concerned about is to keep on hurrying.

Consequently, the stories that Petrus Steyn had to tell of his experiences in the Kalahari desert were as fatiguing to listen to as if you were actually trekking along with him. And the further he trekked into the desert the more wearisome his narrative became, on account of the interludes getting fewer, there being less buck and less Bushmen the deeper he got into the interior. Even so, we felt that he was keeping on using the same Bushmen over and over again. There was also a small herd of springbok that we were suspicious about in the same way.

You can picture to yourself the scene around one of the fires on the church square in Zeerust. It happened at many Nagmaals. A number of young men and women seated around the fire, and Petrus Steyn, a few years older than the members of his audience, would be talking. And when you saw people's mouths going open, it wasn't in astonishment. They were just yawning.

But there was one reason why the young men and women came to Petrus Steyn, and this reason had nothing to do with his Kalahari stories. But it is one of the things I was thinking about when I spoke about the old days and about the faith that was in the land then. For Petrus Steyn was regarded as a prophet. Sometimes people believed in his prognostications, and sometimes they didn't. But, of course, this made no difference to Petrus Steyn. He didn't care whether or not his prophecies came out. He believed in them just the same. More, even. You would understand what I mean by this if you knew Petrus Steyn.

And Petrus Steyn said that why he went into the Kalahari periodically was in order to get fresh inspiration and guid-

ance in regard to the future. He also said it was written in
the Bible that a prophet had to go into the desert.

"I wonder what the Bushmen thought of Zephaniah,
when he was in the desert," Maans Prinsloo asked, "I
suppose they painted portraits of him, on rocks."

Maans Prinsloo knew that Zephaniah was Petrus Steyn's
favourite prophet.

"I don't know whether Ekron was rooted up, like
Zephaniah said would happen," Petrus Steyn replied, "I
read the Bible right through to Revelations, once, to find
out. But I couldn't be sure if Zephaniah was right or not.
That's where my prophecies are different. When I see a
thing in the Kalahari desert, that thing comes out, no matter
who gets struck down by it"—and Petrus Steyn looked
sternly at Maans Prinsloo—"and no matter how long it
takes."

That was how Petrus Steyn always talked about his
prophecies. And maybe that was the reason why they
believed in him, even when they should not have done so.

Anyway, I can still recall, very clearly, that particular Nagmaal at Zeerust when I first understood in which way
Stoffelina Lemmer came into the story. And I also knew
why Maans Prinsloo and Petrus Steyn were on unfriendly
terms. Stoffelina Lemmer had dark hair, and eyes that had a
far-off light in them when she smiled, and that were strangely shadowed when she looked at you without smiling.
And she had red lips.

Stoffelina Lemmer was much in Maans Prinsloo's company at this Nagmaal. But she was also a great deal with
Petrus Steyn. She was nearly always one of the little group
that listened to Petrus Steyn's Kalahari stories, and even if
Maans Prinsloo was with her, holding her hand, even, it still
seemed that she listened to Petrus Steyn's talk. That is, she
appeared, unlike anybody else, actually to listen, and with
an interest that was not simulated.

Once or twice, also, after the rest of Petrus Steyn's

audience had departed, it was observed that Stoffelina Lemmer remained behind, talking to the prophet. And to judge by the animation of Stoffelina Lemmer's lips and eyes, if they were talking about the future it was not in terms of Petrus Steyn's desert prophecies. Beside the burnt-out campfire they lingered thus, once or twice; Stoffelina and Petrus, with the dull glow of the dying embers on their faces.

It was only reasonable, therefore, that Maans Prinsloo should want to know where he stood with Stoffelina Lemmer. That he was in love with her, everybody knew by this time. It was also known, shortly afterwards, that Maans had asked Stoffelina to marry him. And from the way that Maans Prinsloo walked about, looking disconsolate and making remarks of a slighting nature about the whole of the Kalahari, and not just the parts that Petrus Steyn went into, it was clear to us that Stoffelina Lemmer had not accepted Maans Prinsloo just out of hand.

Then, when it was becoming very tense, this situation that involved two men and a girl, Stoffelina Lemmer found a way out.

"Let Petrus Steyn go out into the desert again, after this Nagmaal," Stoffelina said. "And let him then come back and tell us what he has seen. He will learn in the Kalahari what is to happen. When he comes back he will tell us."

Although he believed in Petrus Steyn's prophecies, in spite of his pretence to the contrary, Maans Prinsloo nevertheless seemed doubtful.

"But, look," he began, "Petrus Steyn is sure to go in just a little distance. And then he will come out and say that Stoffelina Lemmer is going to marry Petrus Steyn, and that . . ."

Petrus Steyn silenced Maans Prinsloo with a look.

"I shall trek into the Kalahari desert," he said. "It will be the longest journey I have ever made into the desert. And whatever I see will be prophecy. And just as I see it I shall come back and announce it. Zephaniah may prophesy wrongly, dishonestly, even . . . Petrus Steyn, never! I am still not satisfied about what Zephaniah spoke against Ekron."

Maans Prinsloo was convinced. And so the matter was decided. We inspanned on the Nagmaal plein at Zeerust and journeyed back to our farms by oxwagon, and shortly afterwards we heard that Petrus Steyn had set out on a long trek into the Kalahari desert.

Nothing remained to be told after that Nagmaal at which it was decided that Petrus Steyn should trek into the Kalahari once more. The story ended when the last red ember turned to ashes in that camp-fire on the Nagmaal plein.

Maans Prinsloo remained nervous for a very considerable period.

Because this time Petrus Steyn went on a trip that was longer than anything he had ever undertaken before. In fact, he trekked right across the Kalahari, right through to the other side, and far into Portuguese Angola. Indeed, it was more than fifteen years before we again heard of him, and then it was indirectly, through some Boers who had trekked into Portuguese territory in order to get away from British rule.

I often wondered if those Boers had ever asked Petrus Steyn what it was that he had trekked away from.

But before that time there were many Nagmaals, one succeeding the other, when Stoffelina Lemmer and Maans Prinsloo sat near each other, in front of the same camp-fire, each one waiting, and each one's heart crowded with different emotions, for the return of Petrus Steyn from the desert.

No, Stoffelina Lemmer never married Maans Prinsloo.

Treasure Trove

The February issue 1947 had been Bosman's last as literary editor of the South African Opinion. *By mid-year he'd published his first novel* Jacaranda in the Night, *translated the Rubaiyat of Omar Kayyam into Afrikaans for the Afrikaanse Kulturele Leserskring and accepted a position as their Cape Town representative.*

It was a misconceived publishing venture; but by the time Bosman returned to Johannesburg in the winter of 1947 Leon Feldberg had amalgamated the South African Opinion *with* Trek. *However he undertook to re-employ Bosman on a regular but modified basis. When Bosman's first collection of short stories* Mafeking Road *was published late in 1947 it was dedicated to Leon Feldberg.* Treasure Trove *appeared in the October issue of* Trek *1948.*

It is queer, (Oom Schalk Lourens said), about treasure-hunting. You can actually find the treasure, and through ignorance, or through forgetting to look, at the moment when you have got it, you can let it slip through your fingers like sand. Take Namaqualand, for instance. That part where all those diamonds are lying around, waiting to be picked up. Now they have got it all fenced in, and there are hundreds of police patrolling what we thought, in those days, was just a piece of desert. I remember the last time I trekked through that part of the country, which I took to be an ungodly stretch of sandy waste. But if I had known that I was travelling through thousands of miles of diamond mine, I don't think I would have hurried so much. And that area wouldn't have seemed so very ungodly, either.

I made the last part of the journey on foot. And you know how it is when you are walking through the sand; how you have to stop ever so often to sit down and shake out your boots. I get quite a sick feeling, even now, when I think that I never once looked to see what I was shaking out. You hear of a person allowing a fortune to slip through his fingers. But it is much sadder if he lets it trickle away through between the leather of his veldskoens.

Anyway, when the talk comes round to fortunes, and so on, I always call to mind the somewhat singular search that went on, for the better part of a Bushveld summer, on Jan Slabbert's farm. We all said, afterwards, that Jan Slabbert should have known better, at his age and experience, than to have allowed a stranger like that callow young Hendrik Buys, on the strength of a few lines drawn on a piece of wrapping paper, to come along and start up so much foolishness.

Jan Slabbert was very mysterious about the whole thing, at first. He introduced Hendrik Buys to us as "a young man from the Cape who is having a look over my farm." These words of Jan Slabbert's did not, however, reveal to us much that we did not already know. Indeed, I had on more than one occasion come across Hendrik Buys, unexpectedly and from behind, when he was quite clearly engaged in looking over Jan Slabbert's farm. He had even got down on his hands and knees to look it over better.

But in the end, after several neighbours had unexpectedly came across Jan Slabbert in the same way, he admitted that they were conducting a search for hidden treasure.

"I suppose, because it's hidden treasure, Jan Slabbert thinks that it has got to be kept hidden from us, also," Jurie Bekker said one day when several of us were sitting in his post-office.

"It's a treasure consisting of gold coins and jewels that were buried on Jan Slabbert's farm many years ago," Neels Erasmus, who was a church elder, explained. "I called on Jan Slabbert—not because I was inquisitive about the treasure, of course—but in connection with something of a theological character that happened at the last Nagmaal, and Jan Slabbert and Hendrik Buys were both out. They were on the veld."

"On their hands and knees," Jurie Bekker said.

The ouderling went on to tell us that Jan Slabbert's daughter, Susannah, had said that a piece of the map which that young fellow, Buys, had brought with him from the Cape, was missing, with the result that they were having difficulty in locating the spot marked with a cross.

"It's always like that with a map of a place where there is buried treasure," Jurie Bekker said. "You can follow a lot of directions, until you come to an old tree or an old grave or an old forked road with cobwebs on it, and then you have to take a hundred paces to the west, and then there's something missing—"

"Neels Erasmus, the ouderling, was talking to Susannah," he said, and his voice sounded kind of rasping. He always liked to be the first with the news. But Jurie Bekker was able to assure us that he had just guessed those details. Every treasure-hunt map was like that, he repeated.

"Well, you got it pretty right," Neels Erasmus said. "There is an old tree in it, and an old forked road and an old grave, I think, and also a pair of men's underpants—the long kind. The underpants seem to have been the oldest clue of the whole lot. And it was the underpants that convinced Jan Slabbert that the map was genuine. He was doubtful about it, until then."

The ouderling went on to say that where this map also differed from the usual run of treasure-trove maps was that you didn't have to pace off one hundred yards to the west in the last stage of trying to locate the spot.

"Instead," he explained, "you've got to crawl on your hands and knees for I don't know how far. You see, the treasure was buried at night. And the men that buried it crawled through the bush on hands and knees for the last part of the way."

We said that from the positions in which we had often seen Jan Slabbert and Hendrik Buys of late, it was clear that they were also on the last part of their search.

Andries Prinsloo, a young man who had all this while

been sitting in a corner on a low riempies-stoel, and had until then taken no part in the conversation, suddenly remarked to Neels Erasmus, (and he cleared his throat nervously as he spoke), that it seemed to him as though the ouderling "and—and Susannah—er—had quite a lot to say to each other." Perhaps it was because he was respectful of our company that Andries Prinsloo spoke so diffidently.

At all events, Andries Prinsloo's remark started us off saying all kinds of things of an improving nature.

"Yes," I said to Neels Erasmus, "I wonder what your wife would have to say if she knew that you went to call at Jan Slabbert's house when only his daughter, Susannah, was at home."

"You went in the morning, because you knew that Jan Slabbert and Hendrik Buys would be outside, then, creeping through the wag-'n-bietjie thorns," Jurie Bekker said. "The afternoons, of course, they keep free for creeping through the haak-doring thorns."

"And what will your wife say if she knew of the subjects you discussed with Susannah?" I asked.

"Yes, all those intimate things," Jurie Bekker continued. "Like about that pair of old underpants. How could you talk to a young, innocent girl like Susannah about those awful old underp——"

Jurie Bekker spluttered so much that he couldn't get the word out. Then we both broke into loud guffaws. And in the midst of all this laughter, Andries Prinsloo went out very quietly, almost as though he didn't want to disturb us. It seemed that that young fellow had so much respect for our company that he did not wish to take part in anything that might resemble unseemly mirth. And we did not feel like laughing any more, either, somehow, after he had left.

When we again discussed Jan Slabbert's affairs in the post office, the treasure-hunt had reached the stage where a gang of kaffirs, under the supervision of the two white men, went from place to place on the farm, digging holes. In some places they even dug tunnels. They found nothing.

We said that it would only be somebody like Jan Slabbert, who was already the richest man in the whole of the Northern Transvaal, that would get all worked up over the prospect of unearthing buried treasure.

"Jan Slabbert has given Hendrik Buys a contract," Neels Erasmus, the ouderling said. "I learnt about it when I went there in connection with something of an ecclesiastical nature that happened at the Nagmaal before last. They will split whatever treasure they find. Jan Slabbert will get two-thirds and Hendrik Buys one-third."

We said that it sounded a sinful arrangement, somehow. We also spoke much about what it said in the Good Book about treasures in heaven that the moth could not corrupt. That was after Neels Erasmus had said that there was no chance of the treasure having been buried on some neighbour's farm, instead, by mistake.

"Actually, according to the map," the ouderling said, "it would appear that the treasure is buried right in the middle of Jan Slabbert's farm, somewhere. Just about where his house is."

"If Hendrik Buys has got any sense," Jurie Bekker said, "he would drive a tunnel right under Jan Slabbert's house, and as far as under his bedroom. If the tunnel came out under Jan Slabbert's bed, where he keeps that iron chest of his—well, even if Hendrik Buys is allowed to take only one-third of what is in there, it will still be something."

We then said that perhaps that was the treasure that was marked on Hendrik Buys' map with a cross, but that they hadn't guessed it yet.

That gave me an idea. I asked how Jan Slabbert's daughter, Susannah, was taking all those irregular carryings-on on the farm. The ouderling moved the winking muscle of his left eye in a peculiar way.

"The moment Hendrik Buys came into the house I understood it all clearly," he said. "Susannah's face got all lit up as she kind of skipped into the kitchen to make fresh coffee. But Hendrik Buys was too wrapped up in the treasure-hunt business to notice, even. What a pity—a nice girl like that, and all."

It seemed that that well-behaved young fellow, Andries Prinsloo, who always took the same place in the corner, was getting more respect for our company than ever. Because, this time, when he slipped out of the post office—and it was just about at that moment, too—he appeared actually to be walking on tiptoe.

Well, I didn't come across Jan Slabbert and Hendrik Buys again until about the time when they had finally decided to abandon the search. They had quarrelled quite often, too, by then. They would be on quite friendly terms when they showed the kaffirs where to start digging another hole. But by the time the hole was very wide, and about ten foot deep, in blue slate, they would start quarrelling.

The funny part of it all was that Hendrik Buys remained optimistic about the treasure right through, and he wouldn't have given up, either, if in the course of their last quarrel Jan Slabbert had not decided the matter for him, bundling him on to the government lorry back to Zeerust, after kicking him.

The quarrel had to do with a hole eighteen foot deep, in gneiss.

But on that last occasion on which I saw them together in the voorkamer, Jan Slabbert and his daughter, Susannah, and Hendrik Buys, it seemed to me that Hendrik Buys was still very hopeful.

"There are lots of parts of the farm that I haven't crawled through yet," Hendrik Buys explained. "Likely places, according to the map, such as the pig-sty. I have not yet crept through the pig-sty. I must remember that for to-morrow. You see, the men who buried the treasure crept for the last part of the way through the bush in the dark." Hendrik Buys paused. It was clear that an idea had struck him. "Do you think it possible," he asked, excitedly, "that they might have crawled through the bush backwards—you know, in the dark? That is something that I had not thought of until this moment. What do you say, Oom Jan, to-morrow you and I go and creep backwards, in the direction of the pig-sty?"

Jan Slabbert did not answer. And Susannah's efforts at keeping the conversation going made the situation seem all the more awkward. I felt sorry for her. It was a relief to us all when Neels Erasmus, the ouderling, arrived at the front door just then. He had come to see Jan Slabbert in connection with something of an apostolic description that might happen at the forthcoming Nagmaal.

I never saw Hendrik Buys again, but I did think of him quite a number of times afterwards, particularly on the occasion of Susannah Slabbert's wedding. And I wondered, in the course of his treasure-hunting, how much Hendrik Buys had possibly let slip through his fingers like sand. That was when the ceremony was over, and a couple of men among the wedding-guests were discharging their mausers into the air—welcoming the bride as she was being lifted down from the Cape-cart by the quiet-mannered young fellow, Andries Prinsloo. He seemed more subdued than ever, now, as a bridegroom.

And so I understood then about the distracted air which Andries Prinsloo had worn throughout that feverish time of the great bushveld treasure-hunt; that it was in reality the half-dazed look of a man who had unearthed a pot of gold at the foot of the rainbow.

The Recognising Blues

Using Bosman's reference to Cape Town and the typewriter on which the manuscript was typed as dating devices, The recognising blues *must have been written after his brief unhappy period as the Cape Town representative of that ill-starred publishing venture in the winter of 1947.*

This is the only story in the whole collection to be drawn from the holdings of the Humanities Research Center at Austin, Texas, where the Bosman papers are presently lodged. In 1961, while on a lecture tour from the University of Texas, Professor Joseph Jones evinced an interest in Bosman and successfully negotiated for the acquisition of his papers on their behalf. Helena Lake, Bosman's widow and copyright-holder and Lionel Abrahams, his unofficial literary executor, agreed to this arrangement only after an appeal through the media failed to yield a local equivalent institution to undertake the responsibility of their preservation. To ensure their safety they were sent to Texas in batches, the last parcel being posted in 1962.

I was ambling down Eloff Street, barefooted and in my shirt-sleeves, and with the recognising blues.

I had been smoking dagga, good dagga, the real rooibaard, with heads about a foot long, and not just the stuff that most dealers supply you with, and that is not much better than grass. When you smoke good dagga you get blue in quite a number of ways. The most common way is the frightened blues, when you imagine that your heart is palpitating, and that you can't breathe, and that you are going to die. Another form that the effect of dagga takes is that you get the suspicious blues, and then you imagine that all the people around you, your best friends and your parents included, are conspiring against you, so that when your mother asks you, "How are you?" every word she says sounds very sinister, as though she knows that you have been smoking dagga, and that you are blue, and you feel that she is like a witch. The most innocent remark any person makes when you have got the suspicious blues seems to be impregnated with a whole world of underhand meaning and dreadful insinuation.

And perhaps you are right to feel this way about it. Is not the most harmless conversation between several human beings charged with the most diabolical kind of subterranean cunning, each person fortifying himself behind barbed-wire defences? Look at that painting of Daumier's, called Conversation Piece, and you will see that the two men and the woman concerned in this little friendly chat are all three of them taking part in a cloven-hoofed rite. You can see each one has got the suspicious blues.

There is also the once-over blues and a considerable variety of other kinds of blues. But the recognising blues doesn't come very often, and then it is only after you have been smoking the best kind of rooibaard boom, with ears that long.

When you have got the recognising blues you think you know everybody you meet. And you go up and shake hands with every person that you come across, because you think you recognise him, and you are very glad to have run into him: in this respect the recognising blues is just the opposite of the suspicious blues.

A friend of mine, Charlie, who has smoked dagga for thirty years, says that he once had the recognising blues very bad when he was strolling through the centre of the town. And after he had shaken hands with lots of people who didn't know him at all, and whom he didn't know either, but whom he *thought* he knew, because he had the recognising blues—then a very singular thing happened to my friend, Rooker Charlie. For he looked in the display window of a men's outfitters, and he saw two dummies standing there, in the window, two dummies dressed in a smart line of gents' suitings, and with the recognising blues

strong on him, Charlie thought that he knew those two
dummies, and he thought that the one dummy was Max
Chaitz, who kept a restaurant in Cape Town, and that the
other dummy was a well-known snooker-player called Pat
O'Callaghan.

And my friend Rooker Charlie couldn't understand how
Max Chaitz and Pat O'Callaghan should come to be standing there holding animated converse in that shop-window.
He didn't know, until that moment, that Max Chaitz and
Pat O'Callaghan were even acquainted. But the sight of
these two men standing there talking like that shook my
friend Rooker Charlie up pretty badly. So he went home to
bed. But early next morning he dashed round again to that
men's outfitters, and then he saw that those two figures
weren't Max Chaitz and Pat O'Callaghan at all, but two
dummies stuck in the window. And he saw then that they
didn't look even a bit like the two men he thought they
were—especially the dummy that he thought was Max
Chaitz. Because Max Chaitz is very short and fat, with a
red, cross-looking sort of a face that you can't mistake in a
million. Whereas the dummy was tall and slender and
good-looking.

That was the worst experience that my friend Rooker
Charlie ever had of the recognising blues.

And when I was taking a stroll down Eloff Street, that
evening, and I was barefooted and in my shirt-sleeves, then
I also had a bad attack of the recognising blues. But it was
the recognising blues in a slightly different form. I would
first make up a name in my brain, a name that sounded
good to me, and that I thought had the right sort of a
rhythm to it. And then the first person I would see, I would
think that he was the man whose name I had just thought
out. And I would go up and address him by this name, and
shake hands with him, and tell him how glad I was to see
him.

And a name I thought up that sounded very fine to me,
and impressive, with just the right kind of ring to it, was the

name Sir Lionel Ostrich de Frontignac. It was a very
magnificent name.

And so I went up, barefooted and in my shirt-sleeves, to
the first man I saw in the street, after I had coined this name,
and I took him by the hand, and I said, "Well met, Sir
Lionel. It is many years since last we met, Sir Lionel Ostrich
de Frontignac."

And the remarkable coincidence was that the man whom
I addressed in this way actually *was* Sir Lionel Ostrich de
Frontignac. But on account of his taking me for a bum—
through my being bare-footed and in my shirt-sleeves—he
wouldn't acknowledge that he really was Sir Lionel and that
I had recognised him dead to rights.

"You are mistaken," Sir Lionel Ostrich de Frontignac
said, moving away from me, "You have got the recognising
blues."

Great Uncle Joris

When Great Uncle Joris *appeared in the December issue of* Trek *1948, although Bosman was also contributing in Afrikaans to* Ruiter *and* Brandwag, *his magazine output had been slender. He had poured his creative energy instead into* Cold Stone Jug, *that autobiographical novel he referred to as "A chronicle: being the unimpassioned record of a somewhat lengthy sojourn in prison."*

For quite a number of Boers in the Transvaal Bushveld the expedition against Majaja's tribe of Bechuanas—we called them the Platkop kafirs—was unlucky.

There was a young man with us on this expedition who did not finish a story that he started to tell of a bygone war. And for a good while afterwards the relations were considerably strained between the old-established Transvalers living in these parts and the Cape Boers who had trekked in more recently.

I can still remember all the activity that went on north of the Dwarsberge at that time, with veld-kornets going from one farm-house to another to recruit burghers for the expedition, and with provisions and ammunition having to be got together, and with new stories being told every day about how cheeky the Platkop kafirs were getting.

I must mention that about that time a number of Boers from the Cape had trekked into the Marico Bushveld. In the Drogedal area, indeed, the recently-arrived Cape Boers were almost as numerous as the Transvalers who had been settled here for a considerable while. At that time I, too, still regarded myself as a Cape Boer, since I had only a few years before quit the Schweizer-Reineke district for the Transvaal. When the veld-kornet came to my farm on his recruiting tour, I volunteered my services immediately.

"Of course, we don't want everybody to go on commando," the veld-kornet said, studying me somewhat dubiously, after I had informed him that I was from the Cape, and that older relatives of mine had taken part in wars against the kafirs in the Eastern Province. "We need some burghers to stay behind to help guard the farms. We can't leave all that to the women and children."

The veld-kornet seemed to have conceived an unreasonable prejudice against people whose forebears had fought against the Xosas in the Eastern Province. But I assured him that I was very anxious to join, and so in the end he consented. "A volunteer is, after all, worth more to a fighting force than a man who has to be commandeered against his will," the veld-kornet said, stroking his beard. "Usually."

A week later, on my arrival at the big camp by the Steenbokspruit, where the expedition against the Platkop kafirs was being assembled, I was agreeably surprised to find many old friends and acquaintances from the Cape Colony among the burghers on commando. There were also a large number of others, whom I then met for the first time, who were introduced to me as new immigrants from the Cape.

Indeed, among ourselves we spoke a good deal about this proud circumstance—about the fact that we Cape Boers actually outnumbered the Transvalers in this expedition against Majaja—and we were glad to think that in time of need we had not failed to come to the help of our new fatherland. For this reason the coolness that made itself felt as between Transvaler and Cape Boer, after the expedition was over, was all the more regrettable.

We remained camped for a good number of days beside the Steenbokspruit. During that time I became friendly with Frikkie van Blerk and Jan Bezuidenhout, who were also originally from the Cape. We craved excitement. And when we were seated around the camp-fire, talking of life in the Eastern Province, it was natural enough that we should find ourselves swopping stories of the adventures of our older relatives in the wars against the Xosas. We were all three young, and so we spoke like veterans, forgetting that our knowledge of frontier fighting was based only on hearsay. Each of us was an authority on the best way of defeating a Xosa impi without loss of life to anybody except the members of the impi. Frikkie van Blerk took the lead in this kind of talk, and I may say that he was peculiar in his manner of expressing himself, sometimes. Unfeeling, you might say. Anyway, as the night wore on, there were in the whole Transvaal, I am sure, no three young men less worried than we were about the different kinds of calamities that, in this uncertain world, could overtake a Xosa impi.

"Are you married, Schalk?" Jan Bezuidenhout asked me, suddenly.

"No." I replied, "but Frikkie van Blerk is. Why do you ask?"

Jan Bezuidenhout sighed.

"It is all right for you," he informed me. "But I am also married. And it is for burghers like Frikkie van Blerk and myself that a war can become a most serious thing. Who is looking after your place while you are on commando, Frikkie?"

Frikkie van Blerk said that a friend and neighbour, Gideon Kotze, had made special arrangements with the veld-kornet, whereby he was released from service with the commando on condition that he kept an eye on the farms within a 20-mile radius of his own.

"The thought that Gideon Kotze is looking after things, in that way, makes me feel much happier," Frikkie van Blerk added. "It is nice for me to know that my wife will not be quite alone all the time."

"Gideon Kotze—" Jan Bezuidenhout repeated, and sighed again.

"What do you mean by that sigh?" Frikkie van Blerk demanded, quickly, a nasty tone seeming to creep into his voice.

"Oh, nothing," Jan Bezuidenhout answered, "oh, nothing at all."

As he spoke he kicked at a log on the edge of the fire. The fine sparks rose up very high in the still air and got lost in the leaves of the thorn-tree overhead.

Frikkie van Blerk cleared his throat. "For that matter," he said in a meaningful way to Jan Bezuidenhout, "you are also a married man. Who is looking after your farm—and your wife—while you are sitting here?"

Jan Bezuidenhout waited for several moments before he answered.

"Who?" he repeated. "Who? Why, Gideon Kotze—also."

This time when Jan Bezuidenhout sighed, Frikkie van Blerk joined in audibly. And I, who had nothing at all to do with any part of this situation, seeing that I was not married, found myself sighing as well. And this time it was Frikkie van Blerk who kicked the log by the side of the fire. The chunk of white wood, which had been hollowed out by the ants, fell into several pieces, sending up a fiery shower so high that, to us, looking up to follow their flight, the yellow sparks became for a few moments almost indistinguishable from the stars.

"It's all rotten," Frikkie van Blerk said, taking another kick at the crumbling log, and missing.

"There's something in the Bible about something else being something like the sparks flying upwards," Jan Bezuidenhout announced. His words sounded very solemn. They served as an introduction to the following story that he told us:

"It was during my grandfather's time," Jan Bezuidenhout said. "My great-uncle Joris, who had a farm near the Keiskama, had been commandeered to take the field in the Fifth Kafir War. Before setting out for the war, my great-uncle Joris arranged for a friend and neighbour to visit his farm regularly, in case his wife needed help. Well, as you know, there is no real danger in a war against kafirs—"

"Yes, we know that" Frikkie van Blerk and I agreed simultaneously, to sound knowledgeable.

"I mean, there's no danger as long as you don't go so near

that a kafir can reach you with an assegai," Jan Bezuidenhout continued. "And, of course, no white man is as uneducated as all that. But what happened to my great-uncle Joris
was that his horse threw him. The commando was retreat-
ing just about then—"

"To reload," Frikkie van Blerk and I both said, eager to
show how well-acquainted we were with the strategy used
in kafir wars.

"Yes," Jan Bezuidenhout went on. "To reload. And there
was no time for the commando to stop for my great-uncle
Joris. The last his comrades saw of him, he was crawling on
his hands and knees towards an aardvark-hole. They did not
know whether the Xosas had seen him. Perhaps the commando had to ride back fast because—"

Jan Bezuidenhout did not finish his story. For, just then, a
veld-kornet came with orders from Commandant Pienaar.
We had to put out the fire. We had not to make so much
noise. We were to hold ourselves in readiness, in case the
kafirs launched a night attack. The veld-kornet also in-
structed Jan Bezuidenhout to get his gun and go on guard
duty.

"There was never any nonsense like this in the Cape,"
Frikkie van Blerk grumbled, "when we were fighting the
Xosas. It seems the Transvalers don't know what a kafir
war is."

By this time Frikkie van Blerk had got to believe that he
actually had taken part in the campaigns against the Xosas.

I have mentioned that there were certain differences between the Transvalers and the Cape Boers. For one thing,
we from the Cape had a lightness of heart which the
Transvalers lacked—possibly (I thought at the time) because
the stubborn Transvaal soil made the conditions of life more
harsh for them. And the difference between the two sections
was particularly noticeable on the following morning, when
Commandant Pienaar, after having delivered a short speech
about how it was our duty to bring book-learning and
refinement to the Platkop kafirs, gave the order to

advance. We who were from the Cape cheered lustily. The Transvalers were, as always, subdued. They turned pale, too, some of them. We rode on for the best part of an hour. Frikkie van Blerk, Jan Bezuidenhout and I found ourselves together in a small group on one flank of the commando.

"It's funny," Jan Bezuidenhout said "but I don't see any kafirs, anywhere, with assegais. It doesn't seem to be like it was against the Xosas—"

He stopped abruptly. For we heard what sounded surprisingly like a shot. Afterwards we heard what sounded surprisingly like more shots.

"These Platkop Bechuanas are not like the Cape Xosas," I agreed, then, dismounting.

In no time the whole commando had dismounted. We sought cover in dongas and behind rocks from the fire of an enemy who had concealed himself better than we were doing.

"No, the Xosas were not at all like this," Frikkie van Blerk announced, tearing off a strip of shirt to bandage a place in his leg from which the blood flowed. "Why didn't the Transvalers let us know it would be like this?"

It was an ambush. Things happened very quickly. It became only too clear to me why the Transvalers had not shared in our enthusiasm earlier on, when we had gone over the rise together, at a canter, through the yellow grass, singing. I was still reflecting on this circumstance, some time later, when our commando remounted and galloped away out of that whole part of the district. To reload, we said, years afterwards, to strangers who asked. The last we saw of Jan Bezuidenhout was after he had had his horse shot down from under him. He was crawling on hands and knees in the direction of an aardvark-hole.

"Like grand-uncle, like nephew," Frikkie van Blerk said, when we were discussing the affair some time later, back in camp beside the Steenbokspruit. Frikkie van Blerk's unfeeling sally was not well-received.

Thus ended the expedition against Majaja, that brought

little honour to the commando that took part in it. There was not a burgher who retained any sort of a happy memory of the affair. And for a good while afterwards the relations were strained between Transvaler and Cape Boer in the Marico.

It was with a sense of bitterness that, some months later, I had occasion to call to mind that Gideon Kotze, the man appointed to look after the farms of the burghers on commando, was a Transvaler.

And when I saw Gideon Kotze sitting talking to Jan Bezuidenhout's widow, on the front stoep of their house, I wondered what the story was, about his grand-uncle Joris, that Jan Bezuidenhout had not been able to finish telling.

The Ferreira Millions

*In the latter part of 1949 Bosman changed his lifestyle radically.
He left* Trek *and became a proof-reader on the* Sunday Express *by
day, conserving his creative energy to write another novel at night.
After abandoning two attempts on the subject of city life he began
the first draft of his second novel on dorp life* Willemsdorp.

In October 1949 Herman Bosman began contributing to the
Forum *magazine; and on 1 April* The Ferreira millions *was his
penultimate Oom Schalk Lourens story to appear in it. A fortnight
later he began his Voorkamer series, of which he turned out one a
week until his death on 14 October 1951. These later formed the
basis for two collections in hard cover.*

Although in many respects The Ferreira millions *resembles*
Treasure trove *(in* Trek *October 1948), these stories were
written at least eighteen months apart: and one must accept that it
was part of Bosman's style to return to a theme several times and
experiment with different ways of telling it.*

Marthinus Taljaard lived in a house that his grandfather had
built on the slope of a koppie in the Dwarsberge (Oom
Schalk Lourens said). It was a big, rambling house with
more rooms than what Marthinus Taljaard needed for just
his daughter, Rosina, and himself. Marthinus Taljaard was
known as the richest man in the whole of the Dwarsberge.
It was these two circumstances that led to the koppie around
his house becoming hollowed out with tunnels like the nest
of a white ant.

Only a man who, like Marthinus Taljaard, already had
more possessions in cattle and money than he knew what to
do with, would still want more. That was why he listened
to the story that Giel Bothma came all the way from
Johannesburg to tell him about the Ferreira millions.

Of course, any Marico farmer would have been interested

to hear what a young man in city clothes had to say, talking fast, about the meaning of a piece of yellow paper with lines and words on it, that he held in his hand. If Giel Bothma had come to me in that way, I would have listened to him, also. We would have sat on the stoep, drinking coffee. And I would have told him that it was a good story. I would also have shown him, if he was a young man willing to learn, how he could improve on it. Furthermore, I would have told him a few stories of my own, by way of guidance to him as to how to tell a story.

But towards milking time I would have to leave that young man sitting on the stoep, the while I went out to see what was happening in the cattle-kraal.

That was where Marthinus Taljaard, because he was the wealthiest man in die Dwarsberge, was different. He listened to Giel Bothma's story about the Ferreira millions from the early part of the forenoon onwards. He listened with his mouth open. And when it came to milking time, he invited Giel Bothma over to the kraal with him, with Giel Bothma still talking. And when it came to the time for feeding the pigs, Giel Bothma helped to carry a heavy bucket of swill to the troughs, without seeming to notice the looks of surprise on the faces of the Bechuana farm labourers.

A little later, when Giel Bothma saw what the leaking bucket of swill had done to the legs of his smoothly-pressed trousers, he spoke a lot more. And what he used were not just all city words, either.

Anyway, the result of Giel Bothma's visit from Johannesburg was that he convinced Marthinus Taljaard, by means of the words and lines on that bit of yellow paper, that the Ferreira millions, a treasure comprised of gold and diamonds and elephant tusks, was buried on his farm.

We in the Marico had, needless to say, never heard of the Ferreira millions before. We knew only that Ferreira was a good Afrikaner name. And we often sang that old song,

"Vat jou goed en trek, Ferreira"—meaning to journey northwards out of the Cape to get away from English rule. Moreover, there was the Hans Ferreira family. They were Doppers and lived near Enzelsberg. But when you saw Hans Ferreira at the Indian store at Ramoutsa, lifting a few sheep-skins out of his donkey-cart and trying to exchange them for coffee and sugar, then you could not help greeting with a certain measure of amusement the idea conveyed by the words, "Ferreira millions".

These were the matters that we discussed one midday while we were sitting around in Jurie Steyn's post office, waiting for our letters from Zeerust.

Marthinus Taljaard and his daughter, Rosina, had come to the post office, leaving Giel Bothma alone on the farm to work out, with the help of his yellowed map and the kafirs; the place where to dig the tunnel.

"This map with the Ferreira millions in gold and diamonds and elephant tusks," Marthinus Taljaard said, pompously, sitting forward on Jurie Steyn's riempiestoel, "was made many years ago—before my grandfather's time', even. That's why it is so yellow. Giel Bothma got hold of it just by accident. And the map shows clearly that the Portuguese explorer, Ferreira, buried his treasure somewhere in that koppie in the middle of my farm."

"Anyway, that piece of paper is yellow enough," Jurie Steyn said with a slight sneer. "That paper is yellower than the iron pyrites that a prospector found at Witfontein so it must be gold, all right. And I can also see that it is gold, from the way you hang on to it."

Several of us laughed, then.

"But I can't imagine there being such a thing as the Ferriera millions," Stephanus van Tonder said, expressing what we all felt. "Not if you think that Hans Ferreira's wife went to the last Nagmaal with a mimosa thorn holding up her skirt because they didn't have a safety-pin in the house."

Marthinus Taljaard explained to us where we were wrong.

"The treasure was buried on my farm very long ago," Marthinus Taljaard said, "long before there were any white people in the Transvaal. It was the treasure that the Portuguese explorer, Ferreira, stole from the Mtosas. Maybe that Portuguese explorer was the ancestor of Hans Ferreira. I don't know. But I am talking about very long ago, before the Ferreiras were Afrikaners, but were just Portuguese. I am talking of *very* long ago."

We told Marthinus Taljaard that he had better not make wild statements like that in Hans Ferreira's hearing. Hans Ferreira was a Dopper and quick-tempered. And even though he had to trade sheepskins for coffee and sugar, we said, not being able to wait to change the skins into money first, he would nevertheless go many miles out of his way with a sjambok to look for a man who spoke of him as a Portuguese.

And no matter how long ago either, we added.

Marthinus Taljaard sat up even straighter on the riempies-stoel then.

By way of changing the conversation, Jurie Steyn asked Marthinus how he knew for certain that it was his farm on which the treasure was buried.

Marthinus Taljaard said that that part of the map was very clear.

"The site of the treasure, marked with a cross, is twelve thousand Cape feet north of Abjaterskop, in a straight line," he said, "so that's almost in the exact middle of my farm."

He went on to explain, wistfully, that that was about the only part of the map that was in a straight line.

"It's all in Cape roods and Cape ells, like it has on the back of the school exercise books," Marthinus Taljaard's daughter, Rosina, went on to tell us "That's what makes it so hard for Mr. Bothma to work out the Ferreira map. We sometimes sit up to quite late at night, working out sums."

After Marthinus Taljaard and Rosina had left, we said that young Giel Bothma must be pretty slow for a young man. Sitting up late at night with an attractive girl like Rosina

Taljaard, and being able to think of nothing better to do than working out sums.

We also said it was funny that that first Ferreira should have filled up his treasure map with Cape measurements, when the later Ferreiras were in so much of a hurry to trek away from anything that even looked like the Cape.

In the months that followed there was a great deal of activity on Marthinus Taljaard's farm. I didn't go over there myself, but other farmers had passed that way, driving slowly in their mule-carts down the government road and trying to see all they could without appearing inquisitive. From them I learnt that a large number of tunnels had been dug into the side of a hill on which the Taljaard farm-house stood.

During those months, also, several of Marthinus Taljaard's Bechuanas left him and came to work for me. That new kind of work on Baas Taljaard's farm was too hard, one of them told me, brushing red soil off his elbow. He also said that Baas Taljaard was unappreciative of their best efforts at digging holes into the side of the koppie. And each time a hole came to an end, and there was no gold in it, or diamonds or elephant teeth, then Baas Taljaard would take a kick at whatever native was nearest.

"He kicked me as though it was my fault that there was no gold there," another Bechuana said to me with a grin, "instead of blaming it on that yellow paper with the writing on it.

The Bechuana said that on a subsequent occasion, when there was no gold at the end of a tunnel that was particularly wide and long, Marthinus Taljaard ran a few yards (Cape yards, I suppose), and took a kick at Giel Bothma.

No doubt Baas Taljaard did that by mistake, the Bechuana added, his grin almost as wide as one of those tunnels.

More months passed before I again saw Marthinus Taljaard and his daughter in Jurie Steyn's post office. Marthinus was saying that they were now digging a tunnel that he was sure was the right one.

"It points straight at my house," he said, "and where it comes up, there we'll find the treasure. We have now worked out from the map that the tunnel should go up, at the end. This wasn't clear before, because there is something missing—"

"Yes, the treasure," Jurie Steyn said, winking at Stephanus van Tonder.

"No," Rosina interjected, flushing. "There is a corner missing from the map. That bit of the map remained between the thumb and forefinger of the man in the bar when he gave it to Giel Bothma."

"We only found out afterwards that Giel Bothma had that map given to him by crooks in a bar," Marthinus Taljaard said. "If I had known about that at the start, I don't know if I would have been so keen about it. Why I listened was because Giel Bothma was so well-dressed, in city clothes, and all."

Marthinus Taljaard stirred his coffee.

"But he isn't any more," he resumed, reflectively. "Not well-dressed, I mean. You should have seen how his suit looked after the first week of tunnelling."

We had quite a lot to say after Marthinus Taljaard and Rosina left.

"Crooks in a bar," Stephanus van Tonder snorted. "It's all clear to me, now. That tunnel is going to come up right under Marthinus Taljaard's bed, where he keeps his money in that tamboetie chest. I am sure that map has got nothing to do with the Ferreira treasure at all. But it seems a pretty good map of the Taljaard treasure."

We also said that it was a very peculiar way that that crook had of *giving* Giel Bothma the map. With one corner of it remaining in his hand. It certainly looked as though Giel Bothma must have pulled on it, a little.

We never found out how much truth there was in our speculation. For we learnt some time later that Giel Bothma did get hold of the Taljaard fortune, after all. He got it by marrying Rosina. And that last tunnel did come up under a part of Marthinus Taljaard's rambling old house, built on the side of the koppie. It came up right in front of the door of Rosina Taljaard's bedroom.

The Missionary

The missionary *appeared in the January issue 1951 of* Spotlight *magazine followed by* The traitor's wife *in February. The* Voorkamer *series in the* Forum *was already nine months old; but far from considering the Schalk Lourens tales written out,* Spotlight's *editor Brian Lello believed these two stories to be an auspicious start to a whole new* Spotlight *series.*

He was not to know that the punishing schedule Bosman had set himself—proof-reading by day so that he could finish Willemsdorp *by night, except for Thursdays when he wrote one* Forum *piece a week—left little time or strength for other priorities. These were stories (written or rewritten mostly in Afrikaans) for the bilingual magazine* On Parade, *his* Spotlight *material and an anthology of South African English verse for Afrikaanse Pers Boekhandel, on which he and Gordon Vorster had collaborated but were never to complete.*

The missionary explores the same motif as Graven image, *published in English in* On Parade *after Bosman's death.*

That kaffir carving hanging on the wall of my voorkamer (Oom Schalk Lourens said), it's been there many years. It was found in the loft of the pastorie at Ramoutsa after the death of the Dutch Reformed missionary there, Reverend Keet.

To look at, it's just one of those figures that a kaffir wood-carver cuts out of soft wood, like ndubu or mesetla. But because I know him quite well, I can still see a rough sort of resemblance to Reverend Keet in that carving, even though it is now discoloured with age and the white ants have eaten away parts of it. I first saw this figure in the study of the pastorie at Ramoutsa when I went to call on Reverend Keet. And when, after his death, the carving was found in the loft of the pastorie, I brought it here. I kept it

in memory of a man who had strange ideas about what he
was pleased to call Darkest Africa.

Reverend Keet had not been at Ramoutsa very long.
Before that he had worked at a mission station in the Cape.
But, as he told us, ever since he had paid a visit to the
Marico district, some years before, he had wanted to come
to the Northern Transvaal. He said he had obtained, in the
bushveld along the Malopo River, a feeling that here was
the real Africa. He said there was a spirit of evil in these
parts that he believed it was his mission to overcome.

We who had lived in the Marico for the greater part of
our lives wondered what we had done to him.

On his previous visit here Reverend Keet had stayed long
enough to meet Elsiba Grobler, the daughter of Thys Grobler of Drogedal. Afterwards he sent for Elsiba to come
down to the Cape to be his bride.

And so we thought that the missionary had remembered
with affection the scenes that were the setting for his
courtship. And that was why he came back here. So you can
imagine how disappointed we were in learning the truth.

Nevertheless, I found it interesting to listen to him, just
because he had such outlandish views. And so I called on
him quite regularly when I passed the mission station on my
way back from the Indian store at Ramoutsa.

Reverend Keet and I used to sit in his study, where the
curtains were halfdrawn, as they were in the whole pastorie.
I supposed it was to keep out the bright sunshine that
Darkest Africa is so full of.

"Only yesterday a kaffir child hurt his leg falling out of a
withaak tree," Reverend Keet said to me on one occasion.
"And the parents didn't bring the child here so that Elsiba
or I could bandage him up. Instead, they said there was a
devil in the withaak. And so they got the witch-doctor to
fasten a piece of crocodile skin to the child's leg, to drive
away the devil."

So I said that just showed you how ignorant a kaffir was.

They should have fastened the crocodile skin to the withaak, instead, like the old people used to do. That would drive the devil away quick enough, I said.

Reverend Keet did not answer. He just shook his head and looked at me in a pitying sort of way, so that I felt sorry I had spoken.

To change the subject I pointed to a kaffir wood-carving standing on a table in the corner of the study. That same wood-carving you see today hanging on the wall of my voorkamer.

"Here's now something that we want to encourage," Reverend Keet said in answer to my question. "Through art perhaps we can bring enlightenment to these parts. The kaffirs here seem to have a natural talent for wood-carving. I have asked Willem Terreblanche to write to the education department for a text-book on the subject. It will be another craft that we can teach to the children at the school."

Willem Terreblanche was the assistant teacher at the mission station.

"Anyway, it will be more useful than that last text-book we got on how to make paper serviettes with tassels," Reverend Keet went on, half to himself. Then it was as though an idea struck him, "Oh, by the way," he asked, "would you perhaps like, say, a few dozen paper serviettes with tassels to take home with you?"

I declined his offer in some haste.

Reverend Keet started talking about that carving again.

"You wouldn't think it was meant for me, now, would you?" he asked.

And because I am always polite, that way, I said no, certainly not.

"I mean, just look at the top of my body," he said. "It's like a sack of potatoes. Does the top part of *my* body look like a sack of potatoes?"

And once again I said no, oh no.

Reverend Keet laughed, then—rather loudly, I thought—at the idea of that wood-carver's ignorance. I laughed quite loudly, also, to make it clear that I, too, thought that that kaffir wood-carver was very ignorant.

"All the same, for a raw kaffir who has had no training," the missionary continued, "it's not bad. But take that self-satisfied sort of smile, now, that he put on my face. It only came out that way because the kaffir who made the carving lacks the skill to carve my features as they really are. He hasn't got technique."

I thought, well, maybe that ignorant Bechuana didn't know any more what technique was than I did. But I did think he had a pretty shrewd idea how to carve a wooden figure of Reverend Keet.

"If a kaffir had the impudence to make a likeness like that of me, with such big ears and all," I said to Reverend Keet, "I would kick him in the ribs. I would kick him for being so ignorant, I mean."

It was then that Elsiba brought us in our coffee. Although she was now the missionary's wife, I still thought of her as Elsiba, a bushveld girl whom I had seen grow up.

"You've still got that thing there," Elsiba said to her husband, after she had greeted me. "I won't have you making a fool of yourself. Every visitor to the pastorie who sees this carving goes away laughing at you."

"They laugh at the kaffir who made it, Elsiba, because of his poor technique," Reverend Keet said, drawing himself up in his chair.

"Anyway, I'm taking it out of here," Elsiba answered.

I have since then often thought of that scene. Of the way Elsiba Keet walked from the room, with the carving standing upright on the tray that she had carried the coffee-cups on. Because of its big feet that wooden figure did not fall over when Elsiba flounced out with the tray. And in its stiff, wooden bearing the figure seemed to be expressing the same disdain of the kaffir wood-carver's technique as what Reverend Keet had.

I remained in the study a long time. And all the while the missionary talked of the spirit of evil that hung over the Marico like a heavy blanket. It was something brooding and oppressive, he said, and it did something to the souls of men. He asked me whether I hadn't noticed it myself.

So I told him that I had. I said that he had taken the very words out of my mouth. And I proceeded to tell him about the time Jurie Bekker had impounded some of my cattle that he claimed had strayed into his mealie lands.

"You should have seen Jurie Bekker the morning that he drove off my cattle along the government road," I said. "An evil blanket hung over him, all right. You could almost see it. A striped kaffir blanket."

I also told the missionary about the sinful way in which Niklaas Prinsloo had filled in those compensation forms for losses which he had never suffered, even. And about the time Gert Haasbroek sold me what he said was a pedigree Afrikander bull, and that was just an animal he had smuggled through from the Protectorate one night, with a whole herd of other beasts, and that died afterwards of grass-belly.

I said that the whole of the Marico district was just bristling with evil, and I could give him many more examples, if he would care to listen.

But Reverend Keet said that was not what he meant. He said he was talking of the unnatural influences that hovered over this part of the country. He had felt those things particularly at the swamps by the Malopo, he said, with the green bubbles coming up out of the mud and with those trees that were like shapes oppressing your mind when it is fevered. But it was like that everywhere in the bushveld, he said. With the sun pouring down at midday, for instance, and the whole veld very still, it was yet as though there was a high black wind, somewhere, an old lost wind. And he felt a chill in all his bones, he said, and it was something unearthly.

It was interesting for me to hear the Reverend Keet talk like that. I had heard the same sort of thing before from strangers. I wondered what he could take for it.

"Even here in this study, where I am sitting talking to you," he added. "I can sense a baleful influence. It is some form of—of something skulking, somehow."

I knew, of course, that Reverend Keet was not making any underhanded allusion to my being there in his study. He was too religious to do a thing like that. Nevertheless, I felt uncomfortable. Shortly afterwards I left.

On my way back in the mule-cart I passed the mission school. And I thought then that it was funny that Elsiba was so concerned that a kaffir should not make a fool of her husband with a wood-carving of him. Because she did not seem to mind making a fool of him in another way. From the mule-cart I saw Elsiba and Willem Terreblanche in the doorway of the school-room. And from the way they were holding hands I could see they were not discussing paper serviettes with tassels, or any similar school subjects.

Still, as it turned out, it never came to any scandal in the district. For Willem Terreblanche left some time later to take up a teaching post in the Free State. And after Reverend Keet's death Elsiba allowed a respectable interval to elapse before she went to the Free State to marry Willem Terreblanche.

Some distance beyond the mission school I came across the Ramoutsa witch-doctor that Reverend Keet had spoken about. The witch-doctor was busy digging up roots on the veld for medicine. I reined in the mules and the witch-doctor came up to me. He had on a pair of brown leggings and a woman's corset. And he carried an umbrella. Around his neck he wore a few feet of light-green tree-snake that didn't look as though it had been dead very long. I could see that the witch-doctor was particular about how he dressed when he went out.

I spoke to him in Sechuana about Reverend Keet. I told him that Reverend Keet said the Marico was a bad place. I also told him that the missionary did not believe in the cure

of fastening a piece of crocodile skin to the leg of a child
who had fallen out of a withaak tree. And I said that he did
not seem to think, either, that if you fastened crocodile skin
to the withaak it would drive the devil out of it.

The witch-doctor stood thinking for some while. And
when he spoke again it seemed to me that in his answer
there was a measure of wisdom.

"The best thing," he said, "would be to fasten a piece of
crocodile skin on to the baas missionary."

It seemed quite possible that the devils were not all just in
the Marico bushveld. There might be one or two inside
Reverend Keet himself, also.

Nevertheless, I have often since then thought of how almost
inspired Reverend Keet was when he said that there was evil
going on around him, right here in the Marico. In his very
home—he could have said. With the curtains half-drawn
and all. Only, of course, he didn't mean it that way.

Yet I have also wondered if, in the way that he did mean
it—when he spoke of those darker things that he claimed
were at work in Africa—I wonder if there, too, Reverend
Keet was as wide off the mark as one might lightly suppose.

That thought first occurred to me after Reverend Keet's
death and Elsiba's departure. In fact, it was when the new
missionary took over the pastorie at Ramoutsa and this
wood-carving was found in the loft.

But before I hung up the carving where you see it now, I
first took the trouble to pluck off the lock of Reverend
Keet's hair that had been glued to it. And I also plucked out
the nails that had been driven—by Elsiba's hands, I could
not but think—into the head and heart.

Rosser

Rosser, *which returns to the same theme as* The gramophone *(in* Mafeking Road*) and* Old Transvaal story *(in* Unto Dust*) is the only story of this collection drawn from Bosman's Pretoria Central Prison experience on which he based his autobiographical novel* Cold Stone Jug.

Rosser appeared seven years after Bosman's death in the 1958 spring issue of The Purple Renoster, *edited by Bosman's pupil, disciple and unofficial literary executor Lionel Abrahams, who was responsible for the publication of six books drawn from his works. During the dozen or so issues of* The Purple Renoster *(1957-72) Herman Bosman posthumously kept company with writers like Barney Simon, Ahmed Essop, Ruth Miller, Oswald Mtshali, Wally Serote and Ezekiel Mphalele. I think he would have liked that.*

There was one convict in the prison that I saw at intervals on parade. His name was Rosser. He was old and tall and dried-up. He was also very morose. He was doing time for murder. I never saw him speak to anybody. On exercise he always walked grim and toothless and alone. Other convicts told me about Rosser. He was doing a very long stretch for murder. Nobody seemed to know exactly how long. And it was doubtful whether even Rosser knew any more. With the years he had grown soft in the head, they said.

It was a peculiar sort of murder, too, that Rosser was doing time for, they explained. It appeared that, suspecting his wife of infidelity, he had murdered her on the Marico farm where they lived. And he had disposed of the body by burying it under the dung floor of the voorkamer of the house. So much was, perhaps, reasonable. He had murdered his wife, and the first place he could think of burying her was under the floor of the living-room.

He had filled in the hole again neatly and had smeared the floor with nice fresh cow-dung.

But what made the judge raise his eye-brows, rather, was when it was revealed in court that Rosser had held a dance in that same voorkamer on the evening of the very day on which he had performed those simple sacrificial and funeral rites—whereby his hands got twice stained.

There was a good attendance at that bushveld party, which went on a long time, and several of the dancers afterwards declared in court that they were very shocked when they learnt that they had been dancing all night on top of the late Mrs. Rosser's upturned face. It is true that a number of guests were able to salve their consciences to a limited degree with the reflection that they had danced only the simple country measures: they had not gone in for jazz. One girl also said in court, "Oh, well, I just danced lightly."

Nevertheless, the Rosser case provided the local dominee, who was a stern Calvinist, with first-class material on which to base a whole string of sermons against the evils of dancing . . .

The above, more or less, were the facts about Rosser's crime that I was able to glean from fellow-convicts. But there were several features that mystified me.

"But why did he do it?" I asked a blue-coat, "I mean what did he want to go and throw party for—getting all those people to dance on top of his wife's dead body?"

"It's just because he's got no feelings," the blue-coat said. "That's what. Just look at the way his jaw sticks out without teeth in his head. No feelings, that's what."

Another convict, again, would reply to the same question, "Well, I suppose it was to get the floor stamped down again. They gives dances in the bushveld just to stamp the ground down hard."

A third convict would proffer the explanation, "Well, he was damned glad his wife was dead, see?"

There was a distressing lack of uniformity about the answers I got. And then it suddenly struck me that the convicts were, of course, all going by hearsay. Because, when I questioned them on that point, individually, each agreed that he had never spoken to Rosser. Not as much as passed him the time of day, ever. Rosser just wasn't the sort of person you would ever take it into your head to talk to, anyway.

If Rosser's case was as horrifying as all that, I wondered, then why did the Governor-General-in-Council reprieve him? Why wasn't he hanged? That question, too, I once put to a fellow-convict. And the answer I got surprised me not a little.

"I suppose," the convict said, "why Rosser was reprieved was because the Judge put in a recommendation for mercy —because it was such a good party."

In the end, there was nothing else for me to do about it. I had to get the facts from Rosser himself, at first-hand. I had to approach him and talk to him, and put my question to him straight out. That wasn't an easy thing to do. I had to screw up every nerve in my body to get so far as to address him. It took me a little while to work up enough guts to go up to Rosser and say, "Hallo. How do you do?" In fact, it took me about two years.

And when I did get so far as to talk to Rosser, I realised that he was quite harmless. Only, because nobody had spoken to him for so many years, it was with a considerable effort on his part that he was able to enunciate any words at all. And then, when he spoke, I had to turn my face aside. The way his jaw came up and the way his toothless gums got exposed when he struggled with the unfamiliar thing of speech—the sight of it gave me an acute sense of disgust. But, God knows, his story was simple enough.

"I done my wife in with a chopper because she was sweet on another man," Rosser explained, "And I buried her under the floor and all. And then what happens, but when I got everything clean again, a lot of people come in with concertinas and bottles of wine and brandy. It was a surprise party. And I couldn't say, 'Look here, you can't hold a surprise party in my dining-room. I just buried my wife here.' So I just said, 'Welcome, friends. Come in and sing and dance.'"

So there was no more to the whole thing than just that.

"And the man," Rosser went on, in his lewd-gummed wrestling with the strangeness of words, "the man that I thought my wife was sweet on—he was the one that got the neighbours together and said, 'Let us go and have a surprise party at Rosser's place.' And all that night he was looking for my wife. But I dunno . . ."

"Dunno what," I asked with feigned interest, for I was anxious to be off. One conversation with Rosser in a life-time was enough.

"I dunno if my wife ever really was sweet on him," Rosser said. "I mean, now I been in prison 15 years, I dunno. Because I have always been a much better-looking man that what that man is."

The Murderess

The murderess was the first of a series of Bosman stories to appear in Personality *eighteen years after Bosman's death. They were brought to the attention of the editor Robin Short by Victor Mackeson, producer of the first of Patrick Mynhardt's one-man shows drawn from the works of H C Bosman.*

The reference to corundum mining dates The murderess *after Bosman's period as editor of the* Zoutpansberg Review and Mining Journal *in 1943. But the juxtaposition of Bushveld motifs against city ones that preoccupied much of Bosman's last novel* Willemsdorp *suggests that it was written during the last years of his life.*

"One of your best friends, wasn't he, Frans?" Japie Krige asked of me in the Gouspoort post office after I had read the letter. "You knew them both well, didn't you?"

I nodded, recalling a time when there had been a similar letter in the post, but on *that* occasion not addressed to me. I now read the letter from Willem Lemmer's widow again:

> *Dear Frans,*
>   *You will no doubt be much grieved to learn that my husband is no more. During his last days he spoke of you often. Though he fought hard for life he seemed to know the end was coming. Some time before his death Willem said to me: "Stoffelina, I would wish Frans to come here after I am gone that he may take for himself what he would like to have as a remembrance of me."*
>   *I therefore write you of Willem's last wish that concerns you and say that I would be glad if you could come to the farm when you are able.*
>   *Stoffelina Lemmer*
> *P.S.   The funeral was on Friday. Elder Duvehage read from the Gospel of Mark and we sang from Psalm 18 three verses*

and from Hymn 27 the first and last verses. The elder spoke
very beautifully of Willem.

I could not but recall the time when I had seen a very
similar letter, but held in another's hands.

"Not so very old, either, was he?" Japie Krige remarked
when we left the post office together.

I said, no, but it was an unhealthy area, that low-lying
stretch in the fold of the 'Nwati hills.

"If you ask me," Japie Krige replied, "the whole of the
bushveld seems pretty unhealthy. If it's not malaria, it's
leopards or it's—"

Japie Krige was from the city. He and I were partners in a
corundum proposition outside Gouspoort. And in spite of
the way he talked sometimes, decrying the necessarily primitive conditions of our mode of existence, the fact remained that he had adapted himself remarkably well to a life
which, if it was rough, nevertheless offered a physical
freedom of which a city-dweller could know nothing—and
bestowed on the spirit a quality not of breadth but of
intensity. To the mind of one living in the bush, the bush
did strange things. One's imaginative faculties could not but
be stimulated.

"—or it's snakes," Japie Krige went on. "Well, that's
unhealthy enough, if you ask me."

Yet, in the main, with Japie Krige that sort of thing was
just talk. And I suspected that if he were ever presented with
the opportunity of establishing himself in the city again he
would not take advantage of it. I felt that in spite of what he
said the bushveld had got into Japie Krige's blood and that
he would not quit it readily.

We walked down the dusty road of the Bechuana village
of Gouspoort—of which the post office next to the general
store was the most important building—on the way back to
our camp. It was early afternoon. The heat was oppressive.
Vast numbers of goats were sprawled about the place—
lying in the half-shade of thorn-scrub, pressing up against

the wall of the mission station, seeking shelter from the sun
on the cool side of low rocks that cast shadows no more
than a few inches in length. The goats littered the village
like crumpled pieces of newspaper.

We walked round a fat, tawny-coloured sow that lay with
her large litter in the middle of the road.

"Are you going?" Japie Krige asked me. "I could come
with you. If you thought I wouldn't be in the way that is."

The silence of early afternoon lay over the village and
over the veld. From a great distance there came the sound of
a picannin's voice—a herdboy calling his cattle. That sound
seemed part of, and blended integrally with, the stillness.

"I don't know whether I should go," I answered after an
interval of thought. "I really don't know."

The sandy road before us shimmered in the heat. Fragments of bottle glass on an anthill flung back the sun's rays
with a brilliance as piercing as the edges of the shards
themselves.

"I don't mean that you should go to *collect* anything,"
Japie Krige went on, sounding half-apologetic. "I am just
thinking that—well, you know, when it's a case of somebody's death—the death of a close friend—well, you feel
you want to do something, don't you? I don't suggest that
you should go there just to fetch away his watch, say, as a
keepsake."

Japie Krige made that last remark, I knew, to give a
sardonic twist to his words. Like many people with a true
warmth of feeling he drew back from the idea of appearing
sentimental.

I picked up a piece of rusted barbed wire and flung it a
good distance into the veld. Lying where it was on the road,
that barbed wire was a menace to the tyres of any motor
vehicle passing that way. Not that the road was much used,
of course, by any form of mechanical transport.

"Willem Lemmer did have a watch," I said to Japie Krige,
"an old-fashioned gold watch with a chain and with an
enamel painting on the case. The watch should be—"

It was a queer thing. Just on account of my having *thought* of a motor car in connection with that length of barbed wire the spell of the bushveld village's torpor seemed to be lifted from me. The certain knowledge that there *was* that outside world of civilisation and rush and power stations and materialistic progress and cigarette ends lying on pavements—all this freed me for a while from a hypnotic power whose true nature I understood only too well and from whose horror I recoiled almost as unthinkingly as I yielded to its fascination. For the feelings that went with a walk along the road through a bushveld Bantu village on a hot afternoon formed, I knew, a part of those other, darker feelings that held in them both lure and menace.

"—should be worth quite a good bit," I said to Japie Krige.

"I hope there aren't any snakes here," Japie Krige said as we stood with our suitcases on the tracks of the railway siding, and the train was slowly disappearing from view among the thorn-trees.

Japie Krige surveyed, with marked disfavour, the tangled growths—varying in hue from a diversity of greys to livid greens—through which a footpath looked a good deal like a snake, too, I thought—like a brown mamba even, twisting its way through the grass. I did not, however, mention that to Japie Krige.

There was no one to meet us at the siding. For we had not written to Willem Lemmer's widow that we were coming. Still the Lemmer farmhouse was not many miles distant. It was certainly fewer miles away than one would readily imagine, standing on the railway track and seeing to the east and west a low line of koppies that looked all the more desolate for their intermittent covering of bush and with the northern and southern horizons hidden from view by the immediate trees.

"If they didn't have those koppies there," Japie Krige said, unconsciously speaking as though he were in a city and the koppies were buildings erected by human agency, "then it wouldn't feel quite so lonely. It would be bad enough, I mean. But if you had around you just bush then you could imagine that there is nothing but bush anywhere. But with koppies, there, you can *see* that there is in the whole world nothing but bush."

Japie Krige did not sound very cheerful. He grew even more discouraged when I informed him that those koppies were the 'Nwatis. He remembered what I had told him about how unhealthy the area was. At the same time I said to him that if he was really afraid of snakes we could quit the footpath and take the wagon-road to the Lemmer farm instead. Only it was a longer way round. But Japie said no, we could stick to the footpath.

He said he felt there were worse things in the folds of the 'Nwati hills than snakes. I did not think it necessary to tell him how right he was.

What was singular about my own feelings, I found, was that having once decided to come there the misgivings that obsessed my mind during that afternoon walk through the African village of Gouspoort were suddenly dissipated. Even though there was now no more turning back I felt almost buoyant—even though the way I had to tread was now narrowed to a footpath.

And the fact was that I was not now much concerned with how I felt about things. I was far more interested in Japie Krige's reactions. I could not help but reflect how much they had in common with my own feelings of a former time when I had carried a suitcase down that winding footpath in the company of a man who had a letter that was similar to the letter folded in my breast pocket.

For some distance the way skirted a barbed wire fence. On one hand was the bush, on the other the stubble of mealie land.

I drew Japie Krige's attention to this circumstance.

"That's one thing about Willem Lemmer's widow," I said to Japie. "She doesn't let tragedy overwhelm her. You can

see she's got things on this farm in hand all right. You'd
think that with the boss dead the Bantu would be taking it
easy sitting in front of their huts drinking beer. Or lying by
a stream smoking dagga. But from the quick way they are
a-moving this way and that you'd never think that their
master is in the cold, cold ground."

Japie Krige looked at me in surprise.

"You know, Frans," he said, "the way you're talking it
seems as though you've got no feelings about death."

I replied, trying to sound cryptic, that some day, some
day, perhaps, he would find out, "Only in that case," I
added, "it will be after my time."

It was only when the footpath came to an end and we
emerged into the homestead clearing with the farmhouse at
the end of it that my former trepidation returned. The day
was almost over. From the kraal came shouted words and
the clanking of milk-pails. I looked down. At my feet a
belated ant was scurrying home from work. I found that I
was noticing trivial things again. Once more my spirit was
obsessed with a fear whose cause I knew but whose nature I
could not define for it was a mixed emotion. Inextricably
blended with terror was something that came near to exaltation—but it was exaltation of an unholy sort.

And it was then that Japie Krige took it into his head to
become facetious. I attributed his change of mood to the
relief occasioned in his mind by the sight, in the distance, of
a farmhouse with smoke rising from the chimney, suggest-
ing comfort and human cheer after a journey through miles
of inhospitable bush. Another thing too, I thought, was that
Japie Krige was seeking to imitate my own somewhat
unhappy attempt at a *plaisanterie* of earlier on. Only, when *I*
spoke like that, I said to myself, it was still daylight.

"Not a bad-looking place," was what Japie Krige said.
"Why don't you marry Willem Lemmer's widow? After all,
you've come here for something to remind you of him.
Well, his widow's something he's left behind."

It was on the tip of my tongue to ask Japie Krige why *he*

didn't marry her. But I refrained. Perhaps he would yet, one day. After all, the African bush *was* getting into his blood.

By now it was quite dark. But the gloom could not entirely shroud a fenced-in area to our right in which there were mounds. Not all of the mounds had headstones.

A dove cooed.

Some small creature of the night stirred in the dark green near us.

It seemed to me that my voice sounded exactly as Willem Lemmer's voice had sounded on that first occasion on which he and I had come together to the front door. And now, I used the same words that Willem Lemmer spoke then.

"I got your letter," I said to Stoffelina as she opened the door for us.

I saw at once that she looked more beautiful than ever.

The Question

The question is the second in the Personality *series published eighteen years after Bosman's death. Although the narrator is not identified by his traditional "(Oom Schalk Lourens said)" label, his style is so reminiscent of the way Schalk Lourens* would *have told it, that I cannot mentally assign it to any other raconteur.*

Stefanus Malherbe had difficulty in getting access to the president, to put to him the question of which we were all anxious to learn the answer.

It was at Waterval Onder and President Kruger was making preparations to leave for Europe to enlist the help of foreign countries in the Transvaal's struggle against England. General Louis Botha had just been defeated at Dalmanutha. Accordingly we who were the last of the Boer commandos in the field found ourselves hemmed in against the Portuguese border by the British forces, the few miles of railway line from Nelspruit to Komatipoort being all that still remained to us of Transvaal soil. The Boer War had hardly begun and it already looked like the end.

But when we had occasion to watch from a considerable distance a column of British dragoons advancing through a half-mile stretch of bush country, there were those of us who realised that the Boer War might, after all, not be over yet. It took the column two hours to get through that bush.

Although we who served under Veldkornet Stefanus Malherbe were appointed to the duty of guarding President Kruger during those last days, we had neither the opportunity nor the temerity to talk to him in that house at Waterval Onder. For one thing there were those men with big stomachs and heavy gold watch-chains all crowding around the president with papers they wanted him to sign. Nevertheless when the news came that the English had

broken through at Dalmanutha we overheard some of those
men say, not raising their voices unduly, that something or
other was no longer worth the paper it was written on.
Next morning, when President Kruger again came on the
front stoep of the house, alone this time, we were for the
first time able to see him clearly instead of through the thick
screen of grey smoke being blown into his face from
imported cigars.

"Well," Thys Haasbroek said, "I hope the president when
he gets to Europe enlists the right kind of foreigners to
come and fight for the Republic. It would be too bad if he
came back with another crowd of *uitlanders* with big stomachs and watch-chains, waving papers for concessions."

I mention this remark made by one of the burghers at
Waterval Onder with the president to show you that there
was not a uniform spirit of bitter-end loyalty animating the
3 000 men who saw day by day the net of the enemy getting
more tightly drawn around them. Indeed, speaking for
myself, I must confess that the enthusiasm of those of our
leaders who at intervals addressed us, exhorting us to courage, had but a restricted influence on my mind.

Especially when the orders came for the rolling stock to
be dynamited.

For we had brought with us, in our retreat from Magersfontein, practically all the carriages and engines and trucks
of the Transvaal and Orange Free State railways. At first we
were much saddened by the necessity for destroying the
property of our country. But afterwards something got into
our blood which made it all seem like a good joke. I know
that our own little group that was under the leadership of
Veldkornet Stefanus Malherbe really derived a considerable
amount of enjoyment, towards the end, out of blowing
railway engines and whole trains into the air. A couple of
former shunters who were on commando with us would
say things like, "There goes the Cape mail via Fourteen
Streams," and we would fling ourselves into a ditch to
escape the flying fragments of wood and steel. One of them

also used to shout, "All seats for Bloemfontein," or "First
stop Elandsfontein," after the fuse was lit and he would
blow his whistle and wave a green flag. For several days it
seemed that between Nelspruit and Hectorspruit you couldn't look up at any part of the sky without seeing wheels in
it.

And during all this time we treated the whole affair as fun
and the former shunters had got to calling out, "There goes
the nine-twenty to De Aar," against the signals and,
"There's a girl with fair hair travelling by herself in the end
compartment." Being railwaymen, they couldn't think of
anything else to say.

Because the war of the big commandos, and of men like
Generals Joubert and Cronje, was over it seemed to us that
all the fighting was just about done. We did not know that
the Boer War of General de Wet and Ben Viljoen and
General Muller was then only about to begin.

The next order that our veldkornet, Stefanus Malherbe,
brought us from the commandant was for the destruction of
our stores and field guns and ammunition dumps as well.
All we had to retain were our Mausers and horses, the order
said. That did not give us much cause for hope. At the same
time the first of General Louis Botha's burghers from the
Dalmanutha fight began to arrive in our camp. They were
worn out from their long retreat and many of them had
acquired the singular habit of looking round over their
shoulders very quickly, every so often, right in the middle
of a conversation. Their presence did not help to inspire us
with military ardour. One of these burghers was very upset
at our having blown up all the trains. He had been born and
bred in the *gamadoelas* and had been looking forward to his
first journey by rail.

"I just wanted to feel how the thing rides," he said in
disappointed tones, in between trying to wipe off stray
patches of yellow lyddite stains he had got at Dalmanutha.
"But even if there *was* still another train left I suppose it
would be too late, now."

"Yes, I am sure it would be too late," I said, also looking quickly over my shoulder. There was something infectious about this habit that Louis Botha's burghers had brought with them.

Actually, of course, it was not yet too late for there was still a train, with the engine and carriages intact, waiting to take the president out of the Transvaal into Portuguese territory. There were also in the Boer ranks men whose loyalty to the Republic never wavered even in the darkest times. It had been a very long retreat from the Northern Cape Province through the Orange Free State and the Transvaal to where we were now shut in near the Komati River. And it had all happened so quickly.

The Boer withdrawal, when once it got under way, had been fast and complete. I found it not a little disconcerting to think that on one day I had seen the president seated in a spider just outside Paardeberg drinking buttermilk and then on another day, only a few months later, I had seen him sitting on the front stoep of a house at Waterval Onder a thousand miles away, drinking brandy. Moreover, he was getting ready to move again.

"If it is only to Europe that he is going, then it is not so bad," said an old farmer with a long beard who was an ignorant man in many ways, but whose faith had not faltered throughout the retreat. "I would not have liked our beloved president to have to travel all that way back to the Northern Cape where we started from. He hasn't the strength for so long a journey. I am glad that it is only to Russia that he is going."

Because he was not demoralised by defeat, as so many of us were, we who listened to this old farmer's words were touched by his simple loyalty. Indeed the example set by men of his sort had a far greater influence on the course of the war during the difficult period ahead than the speeches that our leaders came round and made to us from time to time.

Certainly we did not feel that the veldkornet, Stefanus

Malherbe, was a tower of strength. We did not dislike him
nor did we distrust him. We only felt, after a peculiar
fashion, that he was too much like the same kind of man
that we ourselves were. So we did not have overmuch
respect for him.

I have said that we ordinary burghers did not have the
temerity to approach the President and to talk to him as
man to man of the matter that we wanted to know about.
And so we hung back a little while Stefanus Malherbe, an
officer on whom many weighty responsibilities reposed, put
out his chest and strode toward the house to interview the
president. "Put out your stomach," one of the burghers
called out. He was of course thinking of those men who
lately had surrounded the president with their papers and
watch-chains and cigars.

And then, when Stefanus Malherbe was moving in the
direction of the *voorkamer* where we knew the president to
be, and when the rest of the members of our *veldkornetskap*
had drawn itself together in a little knot that stood nervously waiting just off the stoep for the president's reply—I
suppose it had to happen that just then a newly-appointed
general should have decided to treat us to a patriotic talk.
Under other circumstances we would have been impressed
perhaps but at the point of time, when we had already
blown up our trains and stores and ammunition dumps, and
had sunk the pieces that remained of the Staat's Artillerie in
the Komati River—along with some papers we had captured in earlier battle—we were not an ideal audience.

We stood still, out of politeness, and listened. But all the
time we were wondering if the veldkornet would perhaps
be able to slip away at the end of the speech and manage to
get in a few words with President Kruger after all. Anyway
I am sure that we took in very little of what the newly
appointed general had to say.

In the end the general realised the position too. We
gathered that he had known he was going to get the
appointment that day and that he had prepared a speech for

the occasion, to deliver before the president and the State Council, but that he had been unable to have his say in the house because of the bustle attendent upon the president's impending departure. Consequently the general delivered his set speech to us, the first group of burghers he encountered on his way out. After he had got us to sing psalm 83 and had adjured each one of us to humble himself before the Lord, the general explained at great length that if we could perhaps not hope for victory, since victory might be beyond our capacity, we could still hope for a more worthy kind of defeat.

We made no response to his eloquence. We did not sweep our hats upward in a cheer. We did not call out, *"Ou perd!"*. We were only concerned with the veldkornet's chances of having a word with the president before it was too late. The general understood, eventually, that our hearts were not in his address and so he concluded his speech rather abruptly. "Some defeats are greater than victories," he said, and he paused for a little while to survey us before adding, "but not this one, I think."

The meeting having ended suddenly like that, Veldkornet Stefanus Malherbe did, after all, manage to get into the *voorkamer* to speak to President Kruger alone. That much we knew. But when he came out of the house, the veldkornet was silent about his conversation with the president. He did not tell us what the president had said in answer to his question. And in the next advance of the English, which was made within that weekend and which took them right into Komatipoort, Veldkornet Stefanus Malherbe was killed. So he never told us what the President had said in answer to his question about the Kruger millions.

Inspector Vermaak's last case

Inspector Vermaak's last case *was the penultimate Bosman story in the* Personality *series. Detectives both from Marshall Square and Pietersburg featured prominently enough in the life of Herman Charles Bosman for him to be tempted to draw their literary equivalents and enjoy poking fun at them, as in the case of Detective Sergeant Brits in* Willemsdorp. *But Inspector Vermaak strikes me as being possessed of a purely literary genetic inheritance with problems of an abstract nature, not to be confused with the kind of human being Bosman could quite easily have breathed life into had he so chosen.*

INSPECTOR VERMAAK MUST DIE . . .

Henry Eggin, the well-known South African mystery-story writer and creator of that famous character in local crime fiction, Inspector Vermaak of Marshall Square, knew that the time had arrived for him to kill off the Inspector. Other writers of thrillers had, in their time, been forced to make the same kind of decision. You need go no further back than Conan Doyle with his Sherlock Holmes, Henry Eggin thought. There you had the same situation exactly.

The murder mystery entitled, *She Fell in the Vaal* which won for Henry Eggin a measure of recognition as an exponent of the genre, also served to introduce Inspector Vermaak to South African readers of crime fiction. And when the author followed up this first success with *On the Floor of the Voorkamer* and *At One Veld Swoop*, it was natural that he should have retained Inspector Vermaak in the rôle of the sleuth.

That was when the trouble started. Only a writer who had been through that same literary mill could know what Henry Eggin suffered. Inspector Vermaak was everything. His name was practically a household word among readers of murder fiction. If it had been America, Inspector Vermaak would have been filmed. He would have had a place only a few seats behind Philo Vance and Perry Mason and Charlie Chan and he would have given radio talks. In England Inspector Vermaak would have enjoyed a more solid sort of fame. He could never had hoped, of course, for the august society of Sherlock Holmes. In Father Brown's company, too, he would probably have felt a trifle ill at ease. Nor could he have aspired to equality, either socially or as regards professional eminence, with Lord Peter Wimsey, say. But he would have been perfectly at home in the company of Joshua Clunk, Inspector French, Bulldog Drummond, Sergeant Cuff and Inspector John Appelby.

Needless to say, Henry Eggin was more than a little proud of the success that had come the way of Inspector Vermaak. He had also got used to being elbowed out of the way by the stalwart Marshall Square police officer each time he had to rush off to some platteland farm or village to investigate a crime that was baffling the local police. Everybody knew Inspector Vermaak by name and reputation. Not everybody was aware of the identity of Henry Eggin as the author. But Henry Eggin did not mind that. How many people, for instance, could tell you, just on the turn, the name of the writer who created the Thin Man? But did that stop Samuel Dashiell Hammett from drawing authorial royalties and emoluments on an impressive scale?

Why Henry Eggin was harassed was just because he was *not* being pushed aside by Inspector Vermaak's broad shoulders as of old—Inspector Vermaak was not the man he had been in the earlier stories. His logic lacked its former incisiveness, his deductions their one-time brilliance. As a result he was no longer sure of his infallibility. He began repeating himself. Even Inspector Vermaak's warmest admirers had to admit that his handling of the situation in his latest story *Death-knell at Nelspruit* bore an uncomfortably weak resemblance to the methods he employed in that earlier masterpiece *Slain on the Kerkplein*.

Sadder still, the deterioration in his deductive prowess was accompanied by a falling off in the finer qualities of his physical courage as well. Indeed in *The Ghoul of Umghululu* Inspector Vermaak had actually tried to shirk a midnight investigation of certain spectral phenomena on the shallow pretext that if he waited until morning he would be better able to see what was going on. Instead of his being all impatience and haste to get to the demon-haunted *poort* first, Inspector Vermaak had actually had to be pushed on from behind by Henry Eggin. That night saw the author tearing up sheet after sheet of paper he had plucked from the typewriter roller. He had to re-write the same paragraph six times before he was able to induce the reluctant inspector to pull on his boots and to proceed toward the scene of the mystery "with one hand thrust deep into a pocket of his overcoat in which reposed his trusty automatic."

Thus it came about that Henry Eggin was sitting in his study on a summer evening, with the door slightly ajar, brooding on the immediate problem of engineering Inspector Vermaak's decease. Again the author's thoughts reverted to the death of Sherlock Holmes at the hands of the villainous Dr Moriarty. You had only to compare the stories in *The Sign of Four* and *The Adventures of Sherlock Holmes*—two of the earliest volumes in the series—with *The Valley of Fear* of *His Last Bow* recording Sherlock Holmes's adventures after his return from the dead—to realise the tragedy of the situation in which Dr Watson and Conan Doyle found themselves in relation to the resurrected Holmes. Conan Doyle was obviously not interested in him any more—a circumstance that Dr Watson was doing his pathetic best to cover up. Sherlock Holmes had lost his touch and there was nothing anybody in this world could do about it. In having the great detective killed off while he still retained some semblance of his erstwhile greatness, Conan Doyle had acted in the kindest way possible. When he yielded to public clamour and brought Sherlock Holmes back to life. Conan Doyle was guilty of a grave literary misdemeanour. Henry

Eggin decided that he himself would be ruthless. He would not make Conan Doyle's mistake. It was going to be curtains for Inspector Vermaak.

You can't go on indefinitely using the same character over and over again . . . how often had Henry Eggin not repeated the same truth to himself? It's inartistic. Half-a-dozen times, yes, all right. Say a dozen times, even. Okay. It saves you a lot of trouble with creating the atmosphere and perhaps even the framework of a new story. But if you keep on with it too long, the same character again and again making his bow to the public, why—you get sick of him, that's all. That was where Edgar Allan Poe was so right—three appearances of Dupin and *adieu*. But then proud Israfel never made an artistic blunder either in the way he lived or the way he died. Now look at W. W. Jacobs. He would have been a far greater writer if he had only pushed the Night Watchman over the side of the wharf while the going was still good, before the Night Watchman had lost the knack of telling a story.

Henry Eggin pulled open a drawer in his desk and took from it a small shiny Spanish automatic which he laid beside the typewriter. For years the sight of that ugly little weapon had served to furnish him with inspiration for his writing. He then thrust a sheet of foolscap paper into the machine and started typing *Death for Inspector Vermaak*. "How's that for a title?" Henry Eggin asked himself. Somehow, he favoured a title on rather more orthodox lines. So he typed *Inspector Vermaak's Last Case*. Yes, that sounded better. He could start off the story with Inspector Vermaak being shot dead without disclosing the identity of the slayer. And from there he could hark straight back to the beginning. Or he could even, right at the commencement, acquaint the reader with the name of the killer and then tell the story in terms of inverted technique. (Austin Freeman had used that method very successfully.)

Then, as always happened when his author started to write about him, Inspector Vermaak walked into the study.

A quick glance over Henry Eggin's shoulder told him what was afoot. Despite the deterioration that had taken place in his powers of late, Inspector Vermaak's brain was still alert enough to take in the significance of the alternative titles which Henry Eggin had typed at the top of the sheet of paper.

The two men reached simultaneously for the automatic. Inspector Vermaak's hand closed on the weapon first. There was a short, violent struggle. Henry Eggin slumped from his chair on to the floor before the report of the revolver had ceased to fill the room.

It was indeed Inspector Vermaak's last case. That was what Inspector Vermaak thought too as, having closed the Yale lock behind him, he set off down the road.

"I wonder what they'll make of Eggin's death?" Inspector Vermaak mused reflectively. "Structurally, it's a bad murder. They could do something with it, perhaps, from the point of view of the *Locked Room* puzzle but that's a bit out of date now. Maybe they'll just say he was killed by a mysterious Chinese."

Inspector Vermaak chuckled.

"Anyway," he said to himself, "bit of a change from a poison unknown to science. Or from an ice-dagger that melts inside the victim. But it breaks the least-likely-suspect rule so in that way it's a murder that doesn't play fair with the reader—*and it's a mystery that only Inspector Vermaak would be able to solve.*"

A Cold Night

In the last of the Personality *series, under the generic title* Bosman fragments, A cold night *was sandwiched between two other brief sketches titled* New elder *and* Shy young man. *The two sketches flanking* A cold night *certainly appear to be fragments of a whole, to which Bosman might possibly have returned one day. On the other hand,* A cold night, *brief though it might be, is complete. It is also an example of one of those games Bosman tended to play with himself, where he hovered between what he lived and what he created. According to Bosman: "If a thing is poetically true then it is true for every aspect of life."* (South African Opinion *October 1945)*

There was something oddly familiar about the low-walled building with the iron roof that loomed up at us through the shadows. On closer inspection it resolved itself into a two-roomed structure of sun-dried brick. It was a cold night and we had been on the road since dawn.

Part of it had been the wrong road with the result that Gawie Oosthuizen was now in no mood for nonsense. He kicked open the door and we entered. One look at the interior of the place made it obvious that it had not been occupied for many years.

"Anyway, it's better than nothing on a night like this," Gawie Oosthuizen said.

He shivered.

"A schoolmaster lived here a long time ago," Gawie Oosthuizen announced when we had fetched in a tree stump and got a fire burning in the primitive hearth in one corner of the front room.

"He must have used this as his kitchen. And the chimney must have gone through that hole there. That is, if there *was*

a chimney—you don't know with teachers. I forget his
name now. But he was pretty mad, I've heard. Lots of
teachers I've noticed . . ."

I reminded Gawie Oosthuizen that I had also, long ago,
been a teacher in the Marico. I said that to stop him from
making sweeping generalisations that might lead to our
both feeling uncomfortable afterwards.

"I don't say all teachers are mad. Or all former teachers
either," Gawie Oosthuizen acknowledged the warmth from
the fire making him gracious. But this one was different.
He used to write a lot of things, too. All rubbish, I've
heard . . ."

All of a sudden Gawie Oosthuizen sat up very straight on
the battered two-foot-high biscuit tin that he had dragged
out of a corner for a seat. I was squatting on the bare floor.

"I just got a feeling like there was a ghost here," Gawie
Oosthuizen said, looking around at the walls from which
the plaster was peeling and on which his high-up shadow
danced. "Not that I believe in ghosts, mind you."

I told him that I didn't either.

It grew colder. The fire started burning low. Neither of
us felt inclined to go into the raw night after fuel. Accordingly, to keep the wind out, Gawie Oosthuizen borrowed
my jacket, which he thrust into a broken window-pane.
That helped a little. Later on he borrowed my scarf. He
pushed it in the aperture under the door with a stick. That
helped a little more.

He then said it was a pity that I didn't have a tie on. My
tie would go just nicely into that slit in the roof where the
galvanized iron had rusted away, Gawie Oosthuizen explained. He stood on the biscuit tin to have a look. The lid
gave under his weight.

"Anyway, this will help too," Gawie Oosthuizen said
when he saw what was inside the biscuit tin.

The bundles of yellowed manuscripts and black-covered
exercise-books of 20 years ago—their bindings eaten away
by termites—made the fire shoot up brightly again.

"Some of the rubbish he must have left behind," Gawie said.

When the last sheets of my juvenilia went into the flames it felt to me, for a brief moment, almost as though there were indeed a pale ghost hovering in the room.

Ramoutsa Road

Ramoutsa Road *appeared under Bosman's post-prison pen-name Herman Malan in the Bosman-Blignaut critical weekly the* New L S D *on 16 May 1931—the same month as his other Schalk Lourens story* The gramophone *appeared in the* Touleier.

Our original reason for saving Ramoutsa Road *for last was that in the event of public opinion resulting in the preservation of these stories in a book of their own, the logical title then seemed* Ramoutsa Road and Some Almost Forgotten Stories. *Eventually, when* Ramoutsa Road *was deleted from the title, we retained this story in the same order for its valid place in the adventure of how these stories* wouldn't *be forgotten. It also seemed the kind of ending Herman Bosman might have liked.*

You'll see that grave by the side of the road as you go to Ramoutsa, Oom Schalk Lourens said.

It is under that clump of withaaks just before you get to the Protectorate border. The kaffirs are afraid to pass that place at night.

I knew Hendrik Oberholzer well. He was a man of God and an ouderling in the Dutch Reformed Church.

Unlike most of the farmers who lived here in those days, Hendrik Oberholzer was never caught smuggling cattle across the line. Perhaps it was because he was religious and wouldn't break the law.

Or else he chose only dark nights for the work. I don't know. I was rather good at bringing cattle over myself, and yet I was twice fined for it at Zeerust.

Hendrik Oberholzer lived on the farm Paradyskloof. When he first trekked in here he was already married and his son Paulus was about 14. Paulus was a lively youngster and full of spirits when there was drought in the land and there was no ploughing to be done.

But when it rained, and they had to sow mealies, Paulus would be sulky for days.

Once I went to Paradyskloof to borrow a sack of cement from Hendrik for a sheep-dip I was building. Paulus was in the lands, walking behind the plough.

I went up and spoke to him and told him about the cement for the sheep-dip. But he didn't stop the oxen or even turn his head to look at me.

"To hell with you and the cement," he shouted.

Then he added, when he got about 15 yards away, "And the sheep-dip."

For some time after that Hendrik Oberholzer and I were not on speaking terms. Hendrik said that he was not going to allow other men to thrash his son.

But I had only flicked Paulus' bare leg with the sjambok. And that was after he had kicked me on the shin with his veldskoen because I had caught him by the wrist and told him that he wasn't to abuse a man old enough to be his father.

Anyway, I didn't get the cement.

Then, a few days before the minister came to hold the Nagmaal, Hendrik called at my house and said we must shake hands and forgive one another. As he was the ouder-ling, the predikant stayed with him for the three days, and if he was at enmity with anybody, Hendrik would not be allowed to take part in the Nagmaal.

I was pleased to have the quarrel settled. Hendrik Ober-holzer was an upright man whom we all respected for his Christian ways, and he also regularly passed on to me the Pretoria newspapers after he had finished reading them himself.

Afterwards, as time went by, I could see that Hendrik was much worried on account of his son. Paulus was the only son of Hendrik and Lettie.

I knew that often Hendrik had sorrowed because the Lord

had given him no more than one child, and yet this one had strange ways. Because of that, both Hendrik and his wife Lettie became saddened.

Paulus had had a good education. His father didn't take him out of school until he was in Standard IV. And for another thing he had been to Sunday School since he was seven.

Also his uncle, who was a builder, had taught Paulus to lay flat stones for stoeps. So, taken all round, Paulus had more than enough learning for a farmer.

But he was not content with that. He said he wanted to learn. Hendrik pointed out to him what had happened to Piet Slabberts. Piet Slabberts had gone to high school, and when he came back he didn't believe in God.

So nobody was surprised when, two months later, Piet Slabberts fell off an ox-wagon and was killed by the wheels going over his head.

But Paulus only laughed.

"That is not at all wonderful," he said. "If an ox-wagon goes over your head you always die, unless you've got a head like a Bushman. If Piet Slabberts didn't die, only then would I say it was wonderful."

Yes, it was sinful of Paulus to talk like that when we could all see that in that happening was the hand of God.

At the funeral the ouderling who conducted the service also spoke about it, and Piet Slabberts' mother cried very much to think that the Lord had taken away her son because He was not satisfied with him.

Anyway, Paulus did less and less work on the farm. Even when the dam dried up, and for weeks they had to pump water for the cattle all day out of the borehole, Paulus just looked on and only helped when his father and the kaffirs could not do any more.

And yet he was 20 and a strong, well-built young man. But there was something in him that was bad.

At first Hendrik Oberholzer had tried to make excuses for his son, saying that he was young and had still to learn wisdom, but later on he spoke no more about Paulus. Hendrik's wife Lettie also said nothing. But there was always sadness in her eyes.

For Paulus was her only child and he was not like other sons. He would often take a piece of paper and a pencil with him and go away in the bush and write verses all day. Of course Hendrik tore up those bits of paper whenever he found them in the house.

But that made no difference. Paulus just went on with his sinful, worldly things, even after the minister had spoken to him about it and told him that no good could come out of writing verses unless they were hymns.

But even then it was foolish. Because in the Dutch Reformed Hymn Book there were more hymns than what people could use.

Instead of starting to work for himself and finding some girl to whom he could get married, Paulus, as I have said, just loafed about. Yet he was not bad-looking, and there were many girls who would have favoured him if he looked at them first, and from them he could have chosen a woman for himself.

Only Paulus took no notice of girls and seemed shy in their company.

One afternoon I went over to Hendrik Oberholzer's farm to fetch over a black sow that I had bought from him. But Hendrik and Paulus had gone to Zeerust with a load of mealies, so that when I got to the house only Hendrik's wife Lettie was there.

I sat down and talked to her for a little while. By-and-by, after she had poured out the coffee, she started talking about Paulus. She was very grieved about him and I could see that she was not far off crying. Therefore I went and sat next to her on the riempies bank, and did my best to comfort her.

"Poor woman. Poor woman," I said and patted her hand. But I couldn't comfort her much, because all the time I had to keep an eye on the door in case Hendrik came in suddenly.

Then Lettie showed me a few bits of paper that she had found under Paulus' pillow. It was the same kind of verses that he had been writing for a long time; all about mimosa trees and clouds and veld flowers and that sort of nonsense.

When I read those things I felt sorry that I didn't hit him harder with the sjambok that day he kicked me on the shin.

"He does not work even as much as a picannin," Hendrik's wife Lettie said. "All day he writes on these bits of paper. I can't understand what is wrong with him."

"A man who writes things like that will come to no good," I said to her, "And I am sorry for you. It is not good the way Paulus is treating you."

Immediately Lettie turned on me like one of those yellow-haird wild-cats, and told me I had no right to talk about her son.

She said I ought to be ashamed of myself and that, no matter what Paulus was like, he was always a much better man than any impudent Dopper who dared to talk about him. She said a lot of other things besides, and I was pleased when Hendrik returned.

But I saw then how much Lettie loved Paulus. Also, it shows you that you never know where you are with a woman.

Then one day Paulus went away. He just left home without saying a word to anybody.

Hendrik Oberholzer was very much troubled. He rode about to all the farms around here and asked if anyone had seen his son. He also went to Zeerust and told the police, but the police did not do much.

All they ever did was to get our people fined for bringing scraggy kaffir cattle across the line. The sergeant at the station was a raw Hollander who listened to everything Hendrik said, and then at the end told Hendrik, after he had written something in a book, that perhaps what had happened was that Paulus had gone away.

Of course, Hendrik came to me, and I did what I could to help him. I went up to the Marico River right to where it flows into the Limpopo, and from there I came back along the Bechuanaland Protectorate border. Everywhere I inquired for Paulus.

I was many days away from the farm, but as there was not much work at the time of the year, with the rains not yet come, it did not matter.

I had hardly got back home when Hendrik called. From his lands he had seen me come through the poort and he had hastened over to see me.

We sat down in the voorkamer and filled our pipes.

"Well, Lourens," Hendrik said, and his eyes were on the floor, "did you hear anything about Paulus?"

It was early afternoon, with the sun shining in through the window, and in Hendrik's brown beard were white hairs that I had not noticed before.

I saw how Hendrik looked at the floor when he asked about his son. So I told him the truth, for I could see then that he already knew.

"The Lord will make all things right," I said.

"Yes, God knows what is best," Hendrik Oberholzer answered. "I heard about . . . They told me yesterday."

Hendrik could not bring himself to say that which we both knew about his son.

For, on my way back along the Bechuanaland border, I had come across Paulus. It was in some Mtosa huts outside Ramoutsa. There were about a dozen huts of red clay standing in a circle amongst the bushes.

In front of each hut a kaffir lay stretched out in the sun with a blanket over him. All day long those kaffirs lie there in the sun, smoking dagga and drinking beer.

Their wives and children sow the kaffir-corn and the mealies and look after the cattle. And with no clothes on, but just a blanket over him, Paulus also lay amongst those kaffirs.

I looked at him only once and turned away, without knowing whether he had seen me, because he was dagga-drunk. The blanket came up only to his waist, so that the rest of his body was naked and red with the sun. Next to him a kaffir woman sat stringing white beads on a piece of copper wire.

That was what I told Hendrik Oberholzer.

"It would be much better if he was dead," Hendrik said to me. "To think that a son of mine should turn kaffir."

That was very terrible. Hendrik Oberholzer was right when he said it would be better if Paulus was dead.

I had known before of low-class Uitlanders going to live in a kraal and marrying kaffir women and spending the rest of their lives sleeping in the sun and drinking bujah. But that was the first time I had heard of that being done by a decent Boer son.

Shortly afterwards Hendrik left. He said no more about Paulus, except to let me know that he no longer had a son. After that I didn't speak about Paulus any more, either.

In a little while all the farmers in the Groot Marico knew what had happened, and they talked much of the shame that had come to Hendrik Oberholzer's family.

But Hendrik went on just the same as always, except that he looked a great deal older, on account of his shoulders beginning to stoop and his hair to turn white.

Things continued in that way for about six months. Or perhaps it was a little longer, I am not sure of the date, although I know that it was shortly after the second time that I had to pay £10 for cattle smuggling.

One morning I was in the lands talking to Hendrik about putting more wires on the fence, so that we wouldn't need herds for our sheep, when a young kaffir on a donkey came up to us with a note.

He said that Baas Paulus had given him that note the night before, and had told him to bring it over in the morning. He also told us that Baas Paulus was dead.

Hendrik read the note. Then he tore it up. I never got to learn what Paulus had written to him.

"Will you come with me, Lourens?" he asked.

I went with him. He got the kaffirs to inspan the mule-cart, and also to put in a shovel and a pick-axe. All the way to the Mtosa huts Hendrik did not speak.

It was a fresh, pleasant morning in Spring. The grass everywhere was long and green, and when we got to the higher ground, where the road twists round the kranz, there was still a light mist hanging over the trees.

The mules trotted steadily, so that it was a good while before midday when we reached the clump of withaaks that, with their tall, white trunks, stood high above the other thorn-trees.

Hendrik stopped the cart. He jumped off and threw the reins to the kaffir in the back seat.

We left the road and followed one of the cow-paths through the bush. After we had gone a few yards we could see the red of the clay huts. But we also saw, on a branch overhanging the foot-path, a length of ox-riem, the end of which had been cut.

The ox-riem swayed in the wind, and at once, when I saw Hendrik Oberholzer's face, I knew what had happened. After writing the letter to his father Paulus had hanged himself on that branch and the kaffirs had afterwards found him there and had cut him down.

We walked into the circle of huts. The kaffirs lay on the ground under their blankets. But nobody lay in front of that hut where, on that last occasion, I had seen Paulus.

Only in front of the door that same kaffir woman was sitting; still stringing white beads on to copper wire. She did not speak when we came up.

She just shifted away from the door to let us pass in, and as she moved aside I saw that she was with child.

Inside there was something under a blanket. We knew that it was Paulus. So he lay the day I saw him for the first time at the Mtosas, with the exception that now the blanket was over his head as well.

Only his bare toes stuck out underneath the blanket, and on them was red clay that seemed to be freshly dried.

Apparently the kaffirs had not found him hanging from the branch until the morning.

Between us we carried the body to the mule-cart.

Then for the first time Hendrik Oberholzer spoke.

"I will not have him back on my farm," he said. "Let him stay out here with the kaffirs. Then he will be here later on, for his child by the kaffir woman to come to him."

But, although Hendrik's voice sounded bitter, there was also sadness in it.

So, by the side of the road to Ramoutsa, amongst the withaaks, we made a grave for Paulus Oberholzer. But the ground was hard.

Therefore it was not until late in the afternoon that we had dug a grave deep enough to bury him.

"I knew the Lord would make it' right," Hendrik said when we got into the mule-cart.